VILLAGES

Robert Inman

LIVINGSTON PRESS

THE UNIVERSITY OF WEST ALABAMA

Library of Congress Control Number: 2025930412

Typesetting and page layout: Joe Taylor, Kelly West
Proofreading: Brooke Barger, Savannah Beams
Kelly West

Cover art: Kelly West

6 5 4 3 2 1

VILLAGES

PROLOGUE

The first thing he heard was a string bass — one long, low note that was so insistent, so constant, that he could feel it, as much as hear it, vibrating at his core.

It must have been a string bass, because he was at a party, maybe a high school reunion, and there was music, and he danced with a girl. He knew her, but she might have been any of several girls in his class. They slow-danced. She nestled against him, his hand strong on her back pulling her to him, and a staggering sense of longing came over him. They danced for a long time, whispering to each other in words that only they could understand. And then, they were jarred suddenly by an alarm, shrill and loud. A fire drill. Everybody started moving, hurrying, jostling and banging against each other, and he and the girl got separated. He was at a wide doorway, the crowd surging around him, pushing him outside. Somehow, the string bass kept playing, that one droning note. He searched frantically, but he couldn't find the girl. Then his heart broke because he realized that the longing was not for the girl, but for the enormity of everything else — his life, what was, what might be, or might never be, or never even be comprehensible.

He woke, sobbing, the drone deeper in him than ever. A nurse hovered over him. "Bad dream?" He blinked. It was all he could do. She placed her hand on his cheek, and the feel of her calmed him a little. He tried to raise his head. It wouldn't come up. "I need…"

But she didn't understand what he needed any more than he did. She was back with a syringe. Before he slipped over the edge he heard her say, "We'll be there in a couple of hours." When he woke again they were landing at Ramstein.

ONE

The stateside hospital was huge — endless hallways that seemed to go nowhere, a cacophony of sounds, people in white and green in a hurry. But Jonas had his little corner. There was the physical space of his bed in the ward, then the wheelchair, as they worked over the places where his body had been violated — but more than that, what he came to think of as his *area* where everything about him existed, body and all the rest. Ever since he joined the Navy, he had been told to *police up your area*. Keep it neat and squared away. So he worked to keep the mind part of his area quiet, to make it, as much as possible, the *absence* of things. For one thing, it helped to deal with the pain, which began to slowly subside as he started to heal. But it was much more than that. He lived a great deal in long, blank silences — not just not thinking, but *unthinking*. He lived in the midst of the bustle of the ward and the exam rooms and the grim intensity of the rehab areas, but he let none of it intrude on his *area*. He kept to himself as much as possible, avoided conversation. There was nobody he wanted to talk to. He told himself he was squared away.

As far as his body, there were no missing parts except for the little finger and ring finger on his left hand, sheared off by one of the rounds that struck him. That round, after removing the fingers, had smacked into his left shoulder, passing a millimeter from his carotid artery and lodging between the artery and clavicle. The other had gone in low on the inside of his right quad and exited at an upward angle through his thigh, shattering the femur and just missing his groin.

There had been surgeries — first in Germany and then again in the States. He understood the basics from his medic training, but when the healing was progressing and his mind was clear enough from the fog of the meds and concussion, he borrowed an anatomy book and went over what they had done to save him. They had sewed all the ruptured stuff back together and put a steel rod in his leg. He would have a permanent limp. He thought, *I almost wasn't here.* And then he thought, *maybe I'm actually not.*

The shrink was a young guy, maybe thirty. Lieutenant Commander Corrigan, making small talk, explained that he had gone to school on a Navy scholarship and was fulfilling his obligation. Jonas took note of that word, *obligation*. Lieutenant Commander Corrigan looked tired, and Jonas figured it had mostly to do with the stacks of folders on his desk and the table behind him, all these guys with missing parts and screwed-up heads that Corrigan was supposed to fix. The office didn't help — drab Navy issue furniture, washed-out fluorescents.

Jonas was still in his wheelchair. Corrigan had cleared a small space on the desk directly in front of him and he had a single folder open, leafing through it while they talked, but he seemed hemmed in by the stacks of folders on either side.

"How's the rehab going?"

"Fine, sir."

"Things healing okay?"

"Seem to be, yes sir."

"Pain?"

"Some. Getting better. Easing off the meds. Sir."

"That's good."

"Thank you, sir."

Corrigan looked down again at the folder. "Do you mind if I call you Jonas?"

"That's okay, sir."

"So if it's okay for me to call you Jonas, you don't have to call me sir.'"

"What should I call you?"

Corrigan shrugged. "'Doc' would be okay. That's what they call *you*, isn't it? 'Doc'? I've never had a corpsman in here before. So we're just a couple of Docs."

"I'm not a doc anymore," Jonas said, "I'm a patient." He held up his bandaged left hand. "And when I get out of here, I'm gonna be a civilian."

Corrigan nodded at the file folder. "Medical discharge. How do you feel about that?"

"They say I'm unfit for duty."

"No, Jonas, that is *not* what they say. They say the nature and effect of your wounds make it…"

"Same thing, isn't it? Guys with missing parts, a corpsman without fingers who can't walk right? Unfit for duty."

"Let's go back to my question. How do you feel about it?"

"I'm okay with it."

"Oh?"

"A-OK. Sir."

"You've had your war."

"That's about it."

"Well," Corrigan said, "for now, you're still in the U.S. Navy, and the Navy wants to help you deal with your situation."

"What situation?"

Corrigan pursed his lips and scrunched his eyebrows. "We want to help you sort through things. The physical, the mental, the emotional. What happened."

"And what's that? Doc?"

Corrigan lifted the file folder a couple of inches, then set it back down. "What you did…what you went through…"

"I don't remember a single thing."

"Dissociative amnesia," Corrigan said. "Inability to remember important aspects of trauma." It sounded like he was reading from a textbook. "It's common after trauma, and usually temporary."

"Temporary."

"Somewhere, Jonas, you remember exactly what happened, every detail of it."

"Then am I a liar?"

"You're protecting yourself. It's perfectly natural."

Jonas laughed, no mirth to it. "Then are you saying I'm two people?"

Corrigan shook his head. "Not exactly that. But there's a disconnect, and that's what we want to help you deal with. We want to help you to re-connect." Corrigan opened the folder again, flipped a couple of pages, then looked up.

"You really don't know what happened?"

"Not a thing."

"Here's what they say you did, Jonas. Your platoon came under fire, took a number of casualties. Disregarding your own welfare — and serious wounds — you rescued five wounded Marines. You were hit twice yourself. Does any of that sound even vaguely familiar?"

"I know I got hit twice. I can tell that every time I move and look at where my fingers used to be. But how it happened? No. Honestly, no."

"You know that your unit commander has recommended you for the Navy Cross."

"Yeah, I heard that." He made a face. "I don't want it."

"What *do* you want, Jonas?"

Jonas sighed. "To get the fuck out of here."

"I can understand that. But getting the fuck out of here doesn't solve anything."

"What does?"

"Dealing with things."

"Look," Jonas said, "whatever they put in that report, it's done, and I lived through it, and I'm okay."

"Do you not *want* to know?"

"As far as I'm concerned, it just doesn't matter."

Corrigan tapped his head. "Somewhere in here, Jonas, you know, and you know you know, and sooner or later you'll have to deal with it. The later it is, the worse it can be."

"You think I've got PTSD."

Corrigan pulled a piece of paper from the folder. "In your initial screening, you were positive in two areas. What we just talked about… avoiding thinking about what happened, avoiding situations that might remind you of it. And then, feeling numb or detached from other people, from activities, from your surroundings."

Jonas shrugged. "Just trying to stay squared away."

"Any nightmares?"

"Some trouble sleeping," Jonas said, "but I've got meds for that. They help."

"Hyper-vigilance? On edge a lot? Sad? Anxious? Depressed?"

"None of that. They just say I'm not paying attention." Another glance down, studying the paper. "They also say you're withdrawn."

"Just trying to keep my shit together."

Corrigan looked at his watch, then put the piece of paper back in the folder. "Tomorrow, you start with a therapist. I'll be keeping tabs on things, and if at any point you feel a need to talk directly to me…" he cut a quick glance at the stack of folders on his left, "…we'll arrange it."

"Thank you," Jonas said, and then added, "Sir."

Charlene Frick, a civilian. She had some stacks of folders too, but not as many as Lieutenant Corrigan. For the first session they just talked. She didn't seem in a hurry to get to anything grim, and that was okay.

Just before his time was up she said, "Your parents…"

"What about them?"

"You're not staying in touch."

"We're not close," he answered.

"But they're concerned about you. They were here right after you came in, stayed for a few days. Do you remember that?"

"No."

"Since then, they've been back, but I'm told you won't see them, won't answer phone calls, don't open letters and packages."

Jonas could feel something lurch in his gut, shit from way back that he needed to keep at bay. "Tell 'em I'm okay. But I don't want to see 'em or talk to 'em. Not right now."

"You're not close."

"Right."

"Can you tell me about that?"

He wished there was a window to look out of. But there was just the walls and a door that stayed shut. "A couple of years ago my father kicked me out of the house. And then I joined the Navy."

"Can you tell me a little more about that, being kicked out?"

"Not much to tell. We had an argument and he kicked me out."

"You were…how old?"

"Senior in high school. Eighteen."

"How did you feel about it?"

"I wasn't surprised. He's an asshole."

"And your mother?"

"She let him."

"You blame her too?"

"I don't blame anybody. It just happened, it's just the way they both are."

"Where did you go?"

"Stayed with a friend until I finished school."

"A classmate?"

"A doctor."

"Can you tell me about him?"

"He was the guy who delivered me. Did all the doctor stuff when I was growing up. Doctor Ainsley."

"So you called him when you were kicked out?"

"He heard. He came and got me. It was just a couple of months until school was done, and then I joined up."

"Someone you trust?"

"He's always had my back."

She kept pressing him, trying to nudge him into his past, but he got tired of it. *Can you tell me about...can you tell me a little about...* Well, no, he couldn't, or wouldn't. It was done. Why dwell on it? He fell back into one-word answers and then not even that, and she let it go.

But the next session, she brought it up again. He parried with her for awhile, then grew weary of it, and decided to just go ahead and tell her some of that way back shit, and maybe that would satisfy her and she would shut the hell up about the rest of it.

Rodney Boulware was the closest thing Copernicus had to a genuine sports celebrity. He played everything in high school, went to Florida on a baseball scholarship, left after his junior year when Cincinnati offered him a pro contract because he had a 98-mile-an-hour fastball to go with a decent slider. He worked his way up through the minors, Double-A in Waterbury one year, Triple-A in Indianapolis the next. At the end of that season, with Cincinnati going to the playoffs and one of the relief pitchers sidelined with a torn hamstring in his push-off leg, they called Rodney to the bigs. He pitched an inning and a half in one game, preserving a Reds win, and two innings in another when they were down five runs and headed back home. The Reds seemed high on him, and he tried not to be too disappointed the next Spring when they shipped him back to Triple-A, telling him it wouldn't be long before he was back with the big club. Then he tore up his shoulder, and when he and Cincinnati finally figured out that it was all over, he came back home to Copernicus to coach the high school team.

Gladys had had an uneven time of it. She grew up with a sizable fortune around her, thanks to Copernicus Manufacturing, which made specialty fabrics, including liners for landfills. When she was twenty-one, just home from college, her father hired a fellow few years older than Gladys — Gordon Laycock — to help him with his expanding business. Her father liked the young fellow's enthusiasm and confident manner, and when Gordon courted Gladys and asked for her hand in marriage, the father was most agreeable. Seven years and a son later, Gordon took over when the father died of a heart attack at a textile convention in Chicago. Took over and proceeded to run the business in the ground. When Gladys's brother, a neuro-surgeon in New Orleans, stopped getting his monthly checks from the business, he came home and started digging. Gordon had stolen and pissed away most of the money — a good bit of it gambling. The neurosurgeon made sure Gordon went to prison and convinced Gladys to divorce him. Also, he shut down Copernicus Manufactur-ing.

The town never quite got over it — a lot of jobs down the tubes, people moving away. Gladys, lone among the family left in Copernicus, stayed mostly out of sight until, within a year of Gor-don's incarceration, she shocked everybody by marrying Rodney Boulware. Her son Byrd was by then twelve years old, and she told friends that Rodney would be a good father, a strong male figure. Her friends said that Gladys had always seemed like the kind of woman who needed direction. A year into the marriage, Jonas was born.

People in town thought Rodney was a charmer — good talker, affable, firm-handed but fair with his baseball teams. He knew a hell of a lot about baseball, and he had his kids doing things they didn't know they could do, and they won a state championship. People loved him for that.

At home, he was ill-tempered, arbitrary, intense. And critical, especially of Jonas, who was skinny and uncoordinated and didn't give a damn about baseball. Rodney loved to argue, or rather to lecture. Disagree with him, and you could count on enduring an hour of relentless harangue, and then days of silent treatment. Then there was Byrd, son of the first marriage, who was thirteen when Jonas was born. Byrd was everything athletically that Jonas wasn't. Byrd became a multi-sport star, and Rodney was all over it, and let Jonas know he didn't come close to measuring up. He wasn't physically abusive — Jonas sometimes wished Rodney would just hit him and get it over with — but he could cut Jonas down to nothing with words, make him feel small and weak and fearful. He learned to hate Rodney with everything in his soul. But also, by the time he was passing adolescence, he developed an exquisite, fine-tuned antenna, the habit of watchfulness, reading people, all the signals. He began to figure that what made Rodney privately bitter and troubled had mostly to do with his lost life. Copernicus was a long way from Cincinnati, and coaching a high school team, successful though he might be, didn't come anywhere close to what might have been.

Rodney sometimes turned his ill temper on Gladys, and Jonas became intensely protective. He couldn't change Rodney, felt powerless to fight back in any overt way. But he could hunker down, stay quiet, not do anything to set him off, and comfort Gladys in small, unobtrusive ways. She never complained. She took direction. There seemed to be a kind of fatalism to her. Jonas came to see that it was a defensive mechanism that worked for Gladys, and so he began to make it his own. He learned to compartmentalize. There was Rodney, and there was everything else. An image popped into his head: Rodney as an outhouse where all the shit was. And then there was the world outside the outhouse. Jonas grew in the determination to keep the shit where it belonged. There was more to life than that.

The only person he talked to about it was Doc Ainsley. Doc seemed to be around a lot, more than just being Jonas's doctor, with once-a-year checkups and the occasional visit for a cut or a cold. Doc was a great reader with a huge library, and when he found that

Jonas also liked to read, he started lending books. He had Jonas reading Hemingway at twelve, Faulkner at fourteen. Jonas didn't always completely understand what he was reading, but he knew when he finished a book like that, he felt somehow different. And what he didn't understand, Doc could help with. Doc would send him home with a couple of books, and when he came to return them, they talked about what Jonas had read, how it made him feel, and then there were a couple of more books to take with him. Jonas came to think of their book times as little islands where ideas danced in the sand. A long way from the outhouse.

Jonas endured Rodney for a great long while before things came to a head. And the reason things finally came to a head, oddly enough, was sports. Golf. Jonas defied Rodney — loudly, openly, in front of a lot of people. And Rodney kicked him out.

"**T**hat's it," Jonas said when he was finished telling Charlene Frick. He was drained, his whole body flushed and feverish. But he was also exhilarated. It was the first time he had ever said this much of it out loud. The Rodney thing had always been there with Doc Ainsley, but it was largely left unsaid. It was enough that the island was there. But now...*I said it, what an incredible fucking asshole my father is, and now I'm free of it.*

"That's all I'm ever gonna say about that," he said to Charlene Frick, "so don't ask."

Charlene studied him for a moment, and then she said quietly, "Jonas, thank you. I know it took a lot. Now that you've said it, how do you feel?"

"About the same," he said.

"What you've just shared with me, it's truly important. You're putting together your history, giving voice to it. Past is prologue. What we're after is re-connecting with your past, all of it, leading up to your combat experience. When we do that, we arrive at the point where the trauma happened, and we can open that up, too."

"You're trying to get me to re-live it," he said. "Well, I can't do it. I'm just a total blank and I have no interest in changing that. I've said as much as I'm gonna about my parents, and I can tell you about joining the Navy, my training, doing my job with the platoon.

Villages

But if what they say about when I got shot up is true…"

"It *is* true," she insisted. "It's all on paper. Eyewitnesses. It's part of your truth, and right now, maybe the most important part. Jonas, you did an extraordinary thing. But that extraordinary thing was also horrific. It almost got you killed. You've got to deal with that on a conscious level. You've got to reconstruct it, so you can see it for what it is…"

That was when he lost it. "Fuck reconstruct!" He slammed his hand on the arm of his chair. "I don't *want* to know! I *won't* know! Doctor Corrigan says there's two of me. Well shit, send me two paychecks. Whoever that other guy is, he ain't bothering me. I've lost him. And I'm gonna leave him lost."

Frick recoiled, eyes wide. But then she took a deep breath and said, "I understand your anger. It's natural. You *should* be angry."

He sat there very still, calming himself, getting himself back in his *area*. It took a minute or so, but he got things squared away, buttoned-down. And then he gave her a big smile that seemed to surprise her. "Angry? Well, I'm pretty pissed off at the bastards who shot me."

"You have a really nice smile," she said. "I just wonder what's behind it."

"Quiet," he said.

It went on while his body healed, and Jonas could tell that Charlene Frick was getting weary with it. She probed and questioned and tried her best, but he made no effort to help her take him where she wanted him to go. He didn't, wouldn't, help. There was a growing air of sadness about her. And why not, he thought. He and all of these other tough cases — limbs gone, bodies disfigured, some of them horribly, psyches blasted, all those folders in her office and Corrigan's. He understood perfectly what they were trying to do, help people make some peace with what was left of themselves. And those who went where he was unwilling to go — re-living horror — it must be a special kind of horror not only for them, but also for Frick and Corrigan and the rest of the mind people. You could listen to the saddest things on earth and you had to go away and hide before you could cry. How could you do that and not become a trauma victim yourself?

There was, in the recesses of his mind, that ancient thing, the need to comfort, to tell Charlene Frick that she was a good and caring person and she shouldn't worry about him, that he was okay. But he didn't. He was through with trying to comfort people, especially if it meant scaring up old ghosts. In shirking that, he knew he was a failure, and he had spent much of his young life fearing failure. But this one, he was willing to live with.

* * * * *

Jonas came over time to think he probably did owe Charlene Frick at least something besides the Rodney business. So he relented a bit and told her about what went on between the time of Rodney and the time he took two bullets.

The lieutenant's name was Hamrick, but word got out soon after he took over the platoon that he had played linebacker at some small college in Montana, and that his nickname was "Hammer," because he liked to hit people. He was linebacker built, square and low to the ground, and he looked perpetually amped-up and pissed-off. Pissed off, he made clear, at the bad guys, the people who shot at them, tried to blow them up, kept them eternally on edge, wondering when and where the next piece of shit would come from. The first time Hammer spoke to the platoon he said, "This thing won't be over until all the bad guys are dead. And killing bad guys is the only job that matters." Okay, Hammer was gonna be aggressive. The question: was he gonna be reckless?

It took a week to find out. They were humping it across an open field, chasing a couple of bad guys when the whole world opened up on them — small arms, RPG's, coming from almost every direction. Two guys got hit — Vandergriff in his right arm, Figueroa in his groin, just below his flak jacket. Jonas Boulware stopped the life from pouring out of them with the stuff he had in his assault pack — compresses, tourniquets, morphine — but when it was over, Vandergriff lost the arm and Figueroa lost his genitals. Through it all, Hammer kept his shit together, got them disengaged and into defensive position, called in air, secured the area so medevac could come and get Vandergriff and Figueroa. But the platoon knew to a man that Hammer had been too eager, in too much of a hurry, and suddenly they had found themselves in a really bad place, exposed and vulnerable, and it could have been even worse. So Vandergriff was minus an arm and Figueroa was minus his nuts, and everybody liked Vandergriff and Figueroa. Word was that Hammer got his ass chewed at company, but nothing changed, especially Hammer. If anything, he looked more amped-up and pissed-off than ever.

It was Lance Corporal Dunhill who finally said it, a couple of days after the ambush, when word came down about Vandergriff and Figueroa. There were several of them — exhausted, filthy, and wasted after a patrol — having some beers, trying to take the edge off. There was beer because it was the birthday of the Marine Corps. Everybody got two beers. By tradition, there should have been rum, but somehow the rum never got past the rear echelon people. Jonas nursed his beer for awhile and finally handed the can to Dunhill, who had already finished his two. Dunhill downed the beer in three swigs, crunched the can in his fist, and tossed it into a corner. Then he said, "That gung-ho motherfucker is gonna be Commandant of the Marine Corps someday, but in the meantime, he's gonna get everybody else's asses shot off."

Everything froze. Not a muscle twitched. There was a long, stunned silence and nobody looked at anybody else, waiting. It lasted until Sergeant Willis spoke up. "Dunhill," he said, "if I ever hear anything like that come out of your mouth again, I will kick your asshole all the way into your throat." Willis was one hard bastard, a lifer on his third deployment, and nobody in the platoon had the nerve or balls to question him about the least thing. He looked around at the others — glaring, icy. "And that goes for the rest of you sonsabitches."

Willis or not, Dunhill had given voice to it, and it was there — a kind of dread that you forced out of your mind and into some hidden gut place when you saddled up and headed out, because if you didn't, if you thought about anything much except keeping your own shit together, you could lose your ass and the guy's next to you. But when the op was over, it was there, a small foul-smelling animal that lurked at your edges, no matter that it violated that most sacred of Marine things, that you never questioned, you just *did*.

And there was the other thing that added to the dread: Hammer didn't listen to his NCO's. Here he was, fresh out of officer candidate school, raw and combat semi-literate, barking orders, doing reckless and impetuous shit, like he had won the Gulf War singlehanded, and acting as if Willis, the battle-tested warrior, was a rival, a threat to his command. Everybody knew they wouldn't have been humping it across that open field like they did if Willis had had anything to do about it. But Willis was a Marine, the one Marine in the platoon that everybody else trusted. And he had gone to bat for Hammer.

Jonas Boulware wasn't a Marine, he was a Navy man. His official job description was *hospital corpsman*, but that was a misnomer because he hadn't seen the inside of a hospital since San Antonio and Del Mar, where he trained. They had taught him the basics of trying to keep people alive when their bodies were ripped open, and toward the end, one of the instructors called him a natural. He wasn't entirely sure what they meant about that. They had run his ass ragged until he was lean and fit and taught him as much as they could about battlefields and what made Marines Marines. They taught him that even if you were in the keeping-guys-alive business, you'd better be ready to use your own weapon to shoot people, because that might be part of keeping your people alive.

When that was done they sent him to a Marine line platoon. He was twenty years old, slightly-built, and when the Marines first looked him over they seemed reluctant to call him the traditional name, "Doc." But after five months of tending wounds, treating everything from blisters to diarrhea, he was Doc Boulware, one of them. But not one of *them*. He was not, and could never be, a Marine. His job was to keep them alive and functional. He did his job and was, he thought, reasonably good at it — saved some, lost a couple who were beyond saving because IED's had blasted the life from them. He feared sometimes for his own life, but never in the heat of the moment. He just did what he was supposed to do.

What he feared most, though, was failure. It was Jonas Boulware's particular wretched lot, something that had become part of his essence long before the U.S. Navy, to feel an abiding fear of failing other human beings, not being able to give them, do for them, what they needed. Not being able to make things okay. And now, after a couple of months of Lieutenant Hammer, he was haunted by the growing notion that he *would* fail, *must* fail, and there was nothing he could do about it.

And that's where the past left him. Between there and now, here in this big hospital building full of misery, there was nothing. And it could goddamn well stay that way.

* * * * *

At their last session, two days before he was discharged, he simply said, "Thank you. I know how hard you tried. But I'm okay. I want you to understand that." But he could tell she didn't believe it.

There was one more visit with Corrigan, who said, "The Veterans Administration takes over now. I want to strongly encourage you to continue with therapy — individual, with a support group, whatever. There are therapeutic techniques, things that work if you give them a chance, and new ones being looked at all the time. There are those two people, Jonas, the one you know and the one you lost. That other one, he's gonna want back in at some point. It will probably be the hardest thing you'll ever do, but open the door."

"Thank you, sir. I'll think about all that, I really will."

"Where are you going now? Home?"

"There's not much there."

"Then where?"

"Sergeant Willis."

TWO

Willis had tried for a couple of weeks to get in touch with him — a letter, then phone calls. Jonas didn't respond. He didn't want any connection with the platoon or anybody in it, alive or dead. But Willis kept trying, and finally Jonas decided to take a call, put an end to it.

"Boulware…Ray Willis." Ray. All that time in the platoon, and Jonas had never known his first name. Willis was the kind you didn't think of as a first-name guy.

"Hi," Jonas said.

"I been trying to reach you."

"Sorry, I…"

"No problem. Look, how's it going?"

"With what, Sergeant?"

"Are you okay?"

"Fine. All healed up. I'm getting out of here in a few days. Discharge."

"And then what?"

"I don't know, see what's next." There was a long silence, and then Jonas couldn't help himself. "How about you, Sergeant?"

"I'm out."

"Of the Marines?"

"Yeah."

"But I thought…"

Willis's voice slammed into the phone. "Not much call for sergeants with one foot, Boulware."

Jonas waited a moment before he said, "I'm sorry."

"Yeah. But that's the breaks." Now, a burst of what Jonas thought might have been an attempt at a laugh. "Live with it, move on. Look, when they spring you loose, I want you to come see me."

It was the last thing he had expected to hear, and it took him a moment to think of something to say. "Sergeant…"

"Ray."

"Okay…Ray…I don't want…the shit that happened…I don't remember it and I don't want to hear about it. They been trying to drag it out of me, but it's completely gone and that's great."

"Understood. Hey, I don't want to stir up any shit either. You were one of my guys, and a good one, and I just want to see you, see that you're doing okay. Look, we're practically on your way home. Got a little place in Jacksonville, not far from the base. Just Juliette and me. Come have dinner, spend the night. We'll keep it light."

"I don't know…Ray."

And then Willis said the one thing that Jonas Boulware couldn't escape. He said, "You owe me that."

Jonas headed down I-95 in a used Honda with some back pay in his pocket, a cell phone, some jeans and knit shirts in a small duffel.

He found himself amped-up, checking everything, the Honda part of a convoy, eyes darting constantly to the roadside, looking for disturbed earth. Air conditioner turned up full blast, but still sweating, pulse racing. He stopped for gas at a Seven-Eleven. Watching everything and everybody, his back against the side of the car. Inside — bottle of water, M&M's, bag of chips in hand. The guy behind the counter was swarthy and bearded. Jonas felt a jerk in his gut, then backed away, leaving the stuff on the counter, and walked out. He pulled the car to the side of the parking lot and sat there for a long time until he calmed down. Everything looked strange and out of place. First-run jitters, he told himself. It would pass.

It wasn't hard to find — a neighborhood of nondescript brick ranches on the edge of Jacksonville, not far from the LeJeune main gate. Bare yard, couple of scraggly shrubs either side of the front door, Jeep Cherokee in the driveway. The carport was littered with boxes, old pieces of furniture. The roof shingles were curling, paint peeling. Nothing looked squared-away here.

It was late afternoon, the April sun fading, the air warm

with the hint of the summer ahead. Guys in the platoon described LeJeune heat in summer as hellish. The armpit of the U.S. military. Dunhill, who had endured a couple of summers, had a theory about why LeJeune was where it was. "The military, they look for the worst goddamn places in the country — heat, rattlesnakes, swamps, monsoons — and they buy up the land and build a base. Watch the weather in the summer and see where the hottest fucking places in the Carolinas are: LeJeune, Fayetteville, Columbia, Parris Island. They figure if you can survive that, you can survive anywhere."

The rest of the guys in the platoon would agree loudly and bitch and moan about military base weather, but Jonas could tell it was a source of pride with them. They had survived those places, and they were Marines. Listening to them, their jokes and mock-dread about the heat, Jonas could almost feel the place, even though he had never been there. It was one place he had said he had no desire to visit. But now, pulling into Willis's driveway behind the Jeep, giving the house a once-over before he turned off the engine and climbed out, here he was. He thought for an instant of backing out, of just leaving and going somewhere else, leaving this thing in the pit of his stomach — dread, was it? — in Jacksonville, North Carolina. But he had said he would come, however reluctantly, and Jonas had an ancient habit of doing what he said he would do, even when it got him in trouble. *Okay. Get this over with. Move on.*

Five minutes into the visit, he was wishing to hell he *had* just left, or never even thought about coming here in the first place. There was no solid ground beneath his feet. Everything was semi-liquid, uncertain, in motion. He felt a little nauseated.

Willis clumped about on crutches, in need of a shave and a haircut, dressed haphazardly in an old pair of camos — one leg tied at the bottom where the stump was — and a USMC tee shirt. But then, to confound all that, he had a big smile and a firm handshake and an air of ramped-up cheerfulness. In the platoon days, he had never once seen Willis smile. He was gruff, curt, intense. He stayed on everybody's butts about keeping weapons clean, game faces on, watching each other's backs. He never wasted or minced words. His mantra was, *If you keep your shit together and do exactly what I tell you, I'll get you through this.* And they believed him, even when they took casualties, because he was on his third deployment and was still in one piece; and even more importantly, they *needed* to believe him. In the end, of course, he hadn't been able to get them — or himself — through it. He had never seemed to give himself an inch, but now, he had turned loose of who he had been. In the months since the Marines he had gone to seed physically, but then there was this jarring goddamn cheerfulness. *Sergeant Willis*, Jonas thought, *is two people* — disconnected, alien, maybe even at each other's throats. *Maybe that's what they were talking about at the hospital.*

Willis's wife, Juliette, was a stark contrast — an inch or so taller than Willis with long brown hair that framed a long face that would have been pretty if not for the forlorn eyes. She was neatly dressed, and she had the inside of the house ship-shape — bright curtains at the windows, everything clean and orderly except for a corner of the living room where there was a leather recliner surrounded by the litter of magazines, cans and bottles, an overflowing ashtray, a few wadded-up items of clothing. He took it all in quickly, the way he had been trained to do, sized it up and thought, *Things are not good here. It's like she's the Marine and he's morphed into some pitiful, ragged-ass pilgrim.* He felt again the urge to bolt. But he took Juliette's cool hand and tried not to stare at her forlorn eyes.

"Where's your bag?" she asked.

"Oh," he stammered. "I can't stay."

She nodded, and her eyes said, *That's good.*

Willis didn't seem disappointed either. Or if he was, it was smothered beneath this avalanche of cheerfulness. It sounded strange, forced, with maybe even a touch of panic in it. He got Jonas a cold beer from the fridge and they went to the back yard — scraggly grass, charcoal grill, weathered picnic table. Jonas carried a platter of steaks and they stood over the grill drinking their beers while Juliette tossed a salad inside.

"So you're okay?" Willis looked him up and down.

Jonas held up his left hand, the place where the two fingers had been, still red and slightly swollen. "Just this. But it's healing okay. The rest, too."

Willis took a swig of beer and set the empty bottle on the picnic table. "Do you still feel 'em? The fingers?"

"Some pain occasionally, but not the fingers themselves."

"I feel my foot all the time. Phantom sensitivity."

"Yeah, I've heard of that."

Willis laughed. "I guess. You're the doc."

There was an Igloo next to the grill and Willis nudged it open with the rubber tip of one of the crutches. It was full of ice and beer bottles. "Get us another one."

Jonas pulled out two beers, twisted off the caps, handed one to Willis. "Looks like you're getting around okay…with the crutches."

"Pain in the ass, Boulware, but I'm getting a new prosthesis next week. Something wrong with the first one, didn't fit quite right. But I'll get the new one and then I'll have something solid down there where I'm feeling the foot."

"Look, Sarge, could you just call me Jonas?"

"Well, hell yeah. Jonas." He clinked his beer bottle against Jonas's. "First name basis. Fuckin' A."

Willis busied himself with the steaks and Jonas took his beer and went inside to see if he could help with anything. Juliette was shredding a head of lettuce on a cutting board next to the sink, hand working rhythmically with a long serrated knife. She didn't look up. "What can I do?" he asked.

"Silverware and napkins in that drawer," she pointed with her knife. "We'll eat out back."

He stood there for a moment holding the knives and forks and paper napkins in his right hand, the neck of the beer bottle with the thumb and two fingers of the left. They had worked on that a lot in rehab as the hand began to heal, learning to use what he had. He had gotten pretty good with it. "I…I hope it's okay, my being here."

She turned finally to look at him. "I hope so too."

"Is he…" he stopped. *Is he what? Nuts?*

"I wanted to get away from here, anyplace but Jacksonville, but Ray won't go." She gave a flip of the knife in the direction of Camp LeJeune, "He's got rehab, a therapist, support group, at the base. But that's not the real reason. He could find all that somewhere else. The reason is, he can't leave his fabulous fucking Marines. I think somewhere in his head is this crazy notion that they might — sometime, for some stupid reason — actually take him back."

"I didn't want to come," Jonas said, "but he was so insistent. And he said, 'You owe me.' I don't know why, but…"

"Because you saved his life."

"I did?"

"You don't know?"

"I don't know a thing about it. It's a total blank."

"Well, Ray knows. He's talked about you ever since he got back. So you're here, and I hope it doesn't screw him up. He's getting a little better — the nightmares, flashbacks — but..." she pointed the knife directly at him, "...I live in fear, Jonas." Fear, yes, he could tell that. And anger. And why not? She was watching Willis out the window behind the sink, flipping the steaks, working on a fresh beer. "I wish to hell you hadn't come. It's too risky. But you're here. So let him thank you for saving his life — that's what he wants to do — and then get the hell out. Okay?"

"Okay. I will." He turned toward the door, then looked back at her. She was hunched over the cutting board, gripping the handle of the knife hard, and he could see the silent tears trickling down her cheek, falling on the lettuce. "I'm sorry," he said, "for all of it. The whole fucking mess."

She didn't say anything else, and after a moment he went back to Ray Willis.

She didn't have much of anything to say as they ate the steaks and salad. It was Ray who kept up a running narrative. He was from New Jersey, Juliette from right here in Jacksonville. They had met when he was fresh out of boot camp, assigned to First Marines at LeJeune. Lived together for awhile, married seven years now, no kids, maybe later. Juliette worked at a bank. They had bought the house after Ray's first deployment when he made sergeant. She had stayed on here through the second and third. Jonas tried to imagine her alone here while Ray went back, and then back again, because he was a Marine and if the Marines wanted to send him places where he could make a wreck of himself, that was okay. And sure enough, he was a wreck — becoming more animated as they ate, attacking the steak, jabbering away, working on another beer and then another, Juliette casting furtive, worried glances at him but saying nothing except to ask Jonas if he wanted another beer. He shook his head. "Gotta drive."

Ray said he didn't have any education past high school, but

he had been looking into classes at the community college. The Marines would pay for everything. Maybe a trade? His father was in the construction business back in New Jersey — houses, mostly — and Ray had worked after school and summers with him. He liked building stuff. So he might think about carpentry, brick-masonry, something like that. But not plumbing. "Only four things you have to know to be a plumber," he said. "Hot on the left, cold on the right, water runs downhill, don't put your fingers in your mouth." He laughed loudly at that and Jonas tried to join in. Juliette was stone-faced. No, not a plumber. And maybe not construction at all. Not anything medical; he had had a bellyful of sick people. Maybe something in computers. The campus wasn't far, and as soon as he got the new foot and learned to handle a car, he could go every day. Meantime, they had some stuff Online. He rattled on nonstop, finishing his steak before Jonas was halfway through. Juliette had barely touched hers. He never asked a thing about Jonas — where he was headed, what he was going to do when he got there, and Jonas couldn't have said anyway. Make up something? There was a blank road out there, no map.

Suddenly Ray ran out of steam. He fell silent, his shoulders slumped, he pushed the empty plate away and hunkered over the table, staring at the double fist he had made of his hands. Juliette touched his arm. "Get you anything?"

He didn't say anything for awhile. Then he pushed himself up from the table, reaching for his crutches. "Gotta pee." And he tottered off to the house, leaving Jonas and Juliette there in silence. He looked at her, and finally she stared back, her forlorn eyes saying, *See?*

"Is he always like this?" Jonas asked.

"Not that bad." And then her eyes seemed to say, *It's you.* And he felt like a bastard. He wanted to say he was sorry, but then he had already said that, and he thought it wouldn't make anybody feel any better about the whole fucking mess, especially himself. After a couple of minutes of silence he stood, meaning to go, just walk around the side of the house and get in the Honda. But then Ray was back, wearing a Marine Corps hoodie over his tee shirt. Jonas thought it was a little warm to be wearing a hoodie.

Juliette rose, gathering plates and silverware. "Let me help,"

Jonas said.

"No," she said firmly. "I've got this. You guys visit a little more. I know you've got to go."

"I need another beer," Ray said when she was gone, and Jonas fetched him one. He pulled hard on it, draining half the bottle before he set it down on the table between them. "Dunhill was right about Lieutenant Hammer," he said.

"Sarge...Ray...look, I don't want to get into any of that. I really oughta go."

He half rose, and then Ray pulled the .45 from under his hoodie and set it on the table next to the beer bottle. "I'm not gonna hurt you, Boulware, but you have got to suck it up and listen. So sit your ass down."

Jonas looked toward the kitchen window. Juliette was busy at the sink. Ray's back was to her, so she couldn't see what was on the table. "Goddamn," he said softly, and then again, "Goddamn." But he eased back onto the bench.

"Dunhill was right, and I shoulda done something. I shoulda stopped him. But I didn't."

"You'da been court martialed," Jonas said.

"It was my platoon, not his. What's a fucking court-martial compared to *my* Marines getting their asses shot off, just like Dunhill said. And Dunhill got his ass shot off."

"Okay," Jonas said, trying to keep his voice even. "I see what you're saying. But you—"

"I failed 'em. I failed you and all the rest of 'em. But I made it and they didn't, because of you."

"Ray, I told you, I don't remember a thing." He could hear his voice rising, but he couldn't do anything about it because his whole body was beginning to twitch.

"That wound in your hip," Ray said. "Went in low, came out high. You know why?"

"No," Jonas said. "No I don't. And I don't..."

"Because you were humped over, carrying me. I'm laying out there in that fucking street with my foot hanging on by a sliver of flesh and I can't do a goddamn thing to help my Marines. I can't even find my fucking weapon. I'm fucking useless, and I know I've failed and I just want to lay there and die, but you, you fucking do-gooder…" Tears were coursing down his cheeks now, but his voice was steel-hard. "…you skinny-assed do-gooder, you had to put me on your shoulder and save me." His voice broke, and he tried to go on but it stuck in his throat and it took him a moment. What finally came out was barely a whisper: "So here I am, Boulware, a wasted piece of shit, a failure, no good to anybody — my wife, the Marine Corps, anybody. And here you are, a stupid ass little Navy shit, and they're probably gonna give you a medal. Marines save Marines, not Navy dickheads. And I fucking hate you for it."

Then he picked up the .45, put it to his temple, and pulled the trigger.

* * * *

He was naked, shivering, sobbing, cowering in the corner of the shower stall, the water beating down on him like thunder, millions of molecules smashing against each other and making a Niagara sound that filled part of his mind. But not all. The rest was fire and brimstone, things and people blowing up, body parts, somebody's head turning to pulp. He was *there, in the middle of it and there was no way to escape.* He gasped for breath, then hoped that maybe he would just stop breathing and it would be over. But that didn't work, so he clutched his knees to him, trying to become so small he would disappear. Trying to get re-lost.

And then the water stopped, and when he opened his eyes he saw Doctor Frank Ainsley standing over him, hand on the faucet. He stared, uncomprehending. "How…" he croaked.

"You called. Don't you remember?" Jonas shook his head. Doc touched his naked shoulder lightly. "Let's get you dried off and in bed. Can you stand up?" Jonas shook his head again. "Well, I'm a decrepit old fart, Jonas, and I can't lift you. So you'll have to help me. Take your time."

After a minute or so, Jonas uncoiled, wincing at the pain in cramped muscles, old wounds, and then crawled out of the shower, across the dingy tiles of the bathroom floor, into a room where there was a bed. Doc helped him pull himself up and park his butt on the edge of the bed. Doc had a towel and dried him off as best he could. Jonas realized he didn't have any clothes on and put one hand over his crotch. "Hell, Jonas, I was the first person to see your tally-whacker when I pulled you out of the womb and into the world. So don't be shy. Here," he handed the towel to Jonas, "you dry that part." He did, and then Doc helped him half-stand while he pulled the covers back and then slide under the sheet and coverlet. The insanity in his head went on non-stop. He began to cry again. Then Doc Ainsley stuck a needle in his arm and it all went away.

"How long did I sleep?"

Doc was in a chair next to the bed. He looked rumpled and weary. "Twenty-two hours."

"You been here?"

"Of course."

Jonas looked around the room, trying to get his bearings, find the boundaries of his area. Shabby furniture, faded curtain at the window, smell of eons of cigarettes. "Where?"

"The Okinawa Motel."

"Okinawa? How…"

"In Jacksonville."

"Oh."

"Do you want to tell me what happened?"

"Ray shot himself. And then I was in the shower. That's all I know."

Doc nodded. "That's enough for now. Maybe later…"

"What *later*? I don't know anything about *later*."

"We'll figure that out. Later. For now, I'm taking you home. To Copernicus."

THREE

It was an old house, a white frame two-story with a wrap-around porch on the bottom and a small balcony off a room on the top. Doc had his medical practice in the two front rooms of the ground floor on either side of the wide hallway — one for waiting, one for examining. That is, what was left of the medical practice. Doc was in his early seventies. His long-time nurse had retired and he hadn't replaced her, but he had kept the door open after a fashion. Don't bother to call for an appointment, just walk on in, and if the doctor is around, he'll see about you. If Doc isn't in, try the younger guy across town or drive to Waylonsville where there is a hospital. If it's something traumatic, call 911. Some still came, mostly folks who Doc had been seeing about for years. Mostly the Medicare crowd, and Doc groused about having to handle the paperwork. Every week or so, he threatened to quit altogether. There was still the faint, familiar smell of chemicals and medicines about the place.

It was the room with the balcony, where Jonas had lived for most of two months after Rodney kicked him out. There was just enough space for a mahogany double bed, matching night stand and chest of drawers, and a small desk. Parts of Jonas were still here: books on the desk, school stuff mostly, a three-volume set of Bruce Catton's Civil War history that Doc had foisted on him, a few items of clothing in the drawers and hanging in the closet, and in a corner by the door to the balcony, his golf clubs. He didn't remember the golf clubs being here when he went off to the Navy. In fact, the last memory he had of them was leaving the bag lying next to the seventh green when he told Rodney to go to go fuck himself.

It was the same room, but there was something different. He opened the balcony door to air things out, then sat for a while on the edge of the bed, trying to figure out the uncertainty of it. He felt raw, fragile, unsteady, unnerved by Ray Willis. And the room didn't help.

"What have you done to the room?" he asked Doc when he went back downstairs.

Doc gave him an odd look. "Nothing. It's exactly the same as the day you left. Except for the golf clubs. Your mother brought 'em over, said she didn't want Rodney giving 'em away. Why do you think the room is different."

"I don't know, it just feels like…not the same. Even if it is."

"Maybe what's different is you."

"Yeah. Maybe that's it."

"Stay as long as you like," Doc said. "You know where everything is. Miranda still comes five days a week — cook, clean, do the laundry. She'll make your bed if you want, but you ought to do that yourself. Get a routine. Rest some, move around some. Read something. I won't bother you, but I'm here. You need something, you ask. If it's reasonable, I'll do my best."

Doc was a smallish man: thinning white hair, weathered face from hours outdoors, much of it on the golf course, a bit stooped at the shoulders — maybe, Jonas thought, from all these years of seeing about people as much as from age itself. He had bright, clear eyes that looked straight into you, even if he couldn't see as well as he once did. He was neat in his person — hair trimmed, freshly shaved every day, clean clothes, even after his wife Evelyn died eleven years ago. He was plain-spoken. Jonas had once heard him tell Mayor Fleetwood Satterfield, who weighed around three hundred pounds and complained of pain in his hips, "Fleetwood, all you need to do is get off your fat ass." For years, he had been the only doctor in Copernicus, still making house calls in the middle of the night until the guy at the driver's license office told him to stop driving after dark. Now, there was the young guy on the other side of town who never made house calls.

"Give yourself some time," Doc said. "I think you need that."

"And what else?"

"I'll make sure nobody bothers you. Later, if you want to help in the office…"

"I don't ever want to do that again."

Doc nodded. "I understand." He paused for a moment,

then said, "Do you mind if I look you over?" When Jonas hesitated, Doc said, "Whatever you're comfortable with."

Jonas shrugged. "It's okay."

So they went to the examining room and closed the door and Jonas took off everything but his boxers and Doc looked him over, stethoscope cold against his skin, taste of the deflector on his tongue. Ears, eyes, reflexes at his knee and bottom of his feet. Deep breath. Cough. Prodding gently here and there. All the old familiar stuff that Doc had been doing for as long as Jonas could remember, until he lingered at the scars. Jonas looked up into Doc's face, and saw to his surprise the glisten in his eyes. "Ummmm," Doc sighed.

"They tried to kill me."

"Yes.

"But they didn't."

"No."

"I don't remember it."

"Any of it?"

"Well, the stuff that happened before I got wounded, or most of it, I know all that. But not..." he touched the place on his chest.

It took Doc a moment to find his voice, and then it was soft but ragged. "If you want to talk about it — now, anytime — I listen pretty good."

Jonas felt his own tears welling up and willed them back down. "Not now." Then, "I've always been able to talk to you."

"Yeah," Doc said, then he smiled. "About anything."

In the moments before sleep, he thought of what had made Doc smile.

He was twelve. He had a wet dream. He had no idea. He woke up to find his pajama bottom sticky and he tossed it in the laundry hamper. That evening Rodney came crashing into his room and flung the pajamas in his face. "Don't ever do that to your mother again!" he bellowed. Then he stomped out, leaving Jonas bewildered, scared, humiliated. Shortly after, he discovered that he could produce the wet stuff without any dream at all. It was fascinating and felt better than anything else in the world, and he couldn't *not* do it, no matter how hard he tried. But then he knew it was wrong —

Rodney had made sure of that — and the more he did it, the more wrong he felt.

Thirteen. In Doc's office for his annual checkup, which Gladys insisted on even when he felt incredibly self-conscious to be there with most of his clothes off. Stretched out on the exam table, wearing nothing but underwear, he got an erection. Doc had his back to him, looking for something in a cabinet, and when he turned back, Jonas was staring in horror at the rising tent in his shorts. He made a fumbling attempt to cover, but Doc said with a smile, "It does that a lot, I'll bet." Jonas just nodded dumbly. "And when it does, you have to see about it." Jonas nodded again. "Anything you want to ask me?"

Jonas' voice was a croak. "I know I'm not supposed to, but…"

"Not supposed to?" Doc said with a snort, "you *are* supposed to."

"You mean…it's okay?"

"It's absolutely necessary. Your body's changing, hormones, producing fluids that build up, need to go somewhere. It's one of the miracles of creation that we figure out, usually quite on our own, how to handle it. No pun intended."

"Then…can I…"

Doc smiled. "Do it in private, don't let it take over your life. But yes, you can and should. It's normal, it's healthy, and you can't do it too much. Don't ever let anybody tell you different. Plus," he smiled again, "it feels like…"

"Like it's coming off," Jonas said, wide-eyed with wonder and relief.

"That's one of the best descriptions I've ever heard," Doc said, and this time he laughed. Jonas laughed with him and then his erection went down.

He thought now of the gift Doc Ainsley had given him that day of his thirteenth year — the feeling of being safe and reassured, given permission to be free, not just of guilt, but of something much wider. If Rodney was wrong about this, maybe he was wrong about a lot of other stuff, too. Maybe he didn't need to feel hemmed in any more, could be his own person, with his own ideas.

So in time he had ventured into the wider world that Doc

had helped him see. But he had come back now damaged in body and soul and wary of that wider world where there were all sorts of IED's buried just beneath the surface. He had once found safe harbor in Doc's old house. Could he again, here or anywhere? He knew that Doc wanted to help. He could trust Doc. But could he trust himself?

* * * * *

He woke from fitful sleep — sweaty, ragged breath, sheets in a tangle — and lay there in the dark trying to figure out what had been nagging at him just beyond consciousness. It was shadowy, unsettling, menacing. But he couldn't seem to bring it into focus. Maybe it was unknowable. The pills gave him a few hours a night, but there was no depth to it, nothing approaching true rest. He perched on the edge of the bed, breathing deeply the way they had told him in the hospital, then got up and moved to the balcony door, opened it, stepped out into the night. He shivered, the air cool on his damp skin, remembered he was naked. It was something of a mild protest, he thought, sleeping naked. The Navy had never let him sleep that way, and when you were with a bunch of Marines who might be jolted from sleep at any minute by people trying to kill you, you slept with most of your clothes on, and your weapon and other shit where you could put your hands on it in an instant.

The thought of it brought on the weariness again. He had thought it would get better when he mended and began to move around and went through rehab and started getting some physical strength back. But this — this wasn't physical at all. It was just a feeling of constantly sinking into something. It eased sometimes, but it never quite left. Here, in this familiar old house, he should feel comfortable. But he didn't.

He took a deep breath, wrapped his arms around his chest, and tried to get focused on something outside himself. Then he looked out into the night and thought, *That's Copernicus out there.*

He dressed in the dark, padded down the stairs barefoot, and sat on the porch steps to put on jogging shoes. Then he walked.

What he knew of the town, beyond his own small place in it, had come mostly from Doc, who was interested in that sort of thing — the how and why of where you lived. It had been here in some form for a long time, a place straddling a main road and tied for much of its history to the farmland that surrounded it. It was the county seat, which drew people, and for a long time there had been Copernicus Manufacturing, which was another magnet.

The closing of the plant had been a stunning disaster, both to the economy and the town's psyche. And since then, Doc said, there had been a long, slow decline. Doc saw it better than most. Most, he thought, didn't seem to take much interest in the how and why. They just lived. Except for Jonas's mother, who seemed to tote Copernicus around on her back.

Down the sidewalk from Doc's house, along the stretch of what passed for residential gentry, except that what had once been gentry was now a mixed bag: homes that appeared kept up, with neat lawns and shrubs and picket fences, interspersed with others that seemed to be sliding in on themselves. Even in the dim light of street lamps, sagging porches cluttered with odds and ends, flaking paint, weeds, doors and windows that looked morose and out of square. Was it like this when he left three years ago, or had there been even more slippage since then?

In the downtown area there were empty storefronts on the main street, across from the courthouse, and several that weren't empty but didn't look like they were really serious about what they were doing. A State Farm office where a hardware store had been, a photography studio replaced by *Yolanda's Tap and Ballet*. A consign-ment shop with a few odds and ends of clothing and furniture in the window, a hot dog place that was only open for lunch. A couple of places that looked more prosperous: Sikes Department Store, where Gladys had always bought their clothes and where Rodney got a discount because he was the local baseball hero; and Poulos's Café, which was about half café and half juke-joint. Poulos did the meat-and-three thing at lunch, and in the evening there was the beer-and-nachos crowd and in a back room, a couple of pool tables, and occasionally, on the weekends, live music. On past the downtown, on the street that became the highway to Waylonsville, there was a Dairy Queen and an OK Tire Store and a Family Dollar and a couple of service stations, and maybe that was what passed for thriving these days, but the downtown itself looked weary and washed-out. Like Jonas.

At Poulos's, he turned around and headed back toward Doc's. He could have turned right at the intersection across from the police station and walked out toward the high school and the house where he used to live, but his leg was hurting now, and besides, the high school and the house where he used to live seemed like ancient history.

As he walked, he thought about what had brought him here. Ray Willis, the Okinawa Motel, Doc to the rescue. If it hadn't happened that way, where would he be now? He had had no plans, no intentions, no direction. A blank page where there might have been a map. He had never meant to be in Copernicus again, not ever in his life. In the months with the platoon, they had all talked and talked and talked, mostly as a way to stay connected to something they had left behind: rad bands, sports teams, wives and girlfriends and hookers. And home. For many of them, it was bittersweet — broken-down marriages, disappointments — but they kept coming back to it. Not Jonas. He could carry on at length on Metallica and Guns 'N Roses and the Atlanta Falcons and Tiger Woods, but not home. It was simply something he had left behind.

Until now. And now, walking this street while it turned pale in the east and the street lamps winked off, it struck him how different it all felt. Not just the sagging homes and empty storefronts, but the *feel* of the place, as if it was skewed at odd angles and out of tune with itself. It was Copernicus, the place where he had been born and raised and educated and had friends and done the kinds of things you did as a kid, the place from which he had ventured into that wider world. Except that it wasn't. It felt foreign. He wondered if this is what a ghost felt like — able to pass through walls, unable to touch anything real. Was the town cockeyed? Or was he?

Two things for sure. He wasn't the Jonas who had left this place three years ago. Doc was right about that. And, he didn't see how in the world he could stay.

He was almost back to Doc's when a panel truck with ladders on the roof passed — the first vehicle he had seen since he left the house — and screeched to a halt just beyond him. The door flew open and out leaped Fred Wesley Satterfield.

"You're back!" Fred Wesley cried, bounding across the sidewalk and enveloping Jonas in a crushing hug. "By gosh, you're back!"

Jonas struggled to keep himself from recoiling. He didn't like to be touched. But he managed to wrap his arms around Fred Wesley and hold on for a minute or so. Then Fred Wesley released him and held him at arm's length. His smile, even here in first light, was dazzling. "Oh boy," he said. "I am mighty glad to see you, Jonas Boulware. I was afraid I might never see you again."

Jonas jammed his hands in his pockets. "Well, here I am."

"Are you okay?"

"Pretty much."

"I been calling your mama all the time, but all she would tell me was that you got hurt over there and you were in a hospital getting fixed up."

"That's pretty much it, Fred Wesley."

"Well," Fred Wesley said gravely, "you can tell me about it, or some of it, or none of it, whatever you want. I can handle it."

"I know you can," Jonas said.

"'Cause I'm still your friend. Even after all this time."

Jonas ducked his head. "I'm sorry I didn't stay in touch."

"You shoulda."

"Yeah. I shoulda."

"But that's okay. 'Cause you're back."

Jonas took his hands out of his pockets and put them on Fred Wesley's shoulders. "And what about you, Fred Wesley?"

"I'm in construction," he grinned. "That's my truck. Well, it belongs to Rayfield, but he lets me drive it."

"Construction?"

"Little bit of everything. Me and Rayfield, we paint, build stuff. Home repairs, that sorta thing. Everything but plumbing. We don't fool with plumbing. You can get yourself in a heap of trouble with plumbing."

Jonas started to tell the joke he'd heard about plumbing… *don't put your fingers in your mouth*…but then he realized where he heard it. Ray Willis. So he didn't. "So," he said instead, "you like construction?"

"Yep," Fred Wesley said. "Especially painting. When you're painting, you can think or not think, whatever suits you. All you got to remember is not to paint the same stuff twice. Unless you're doing two coats. That other stuff, home repairs, you gotta think more or you might cut your fingers off."

"Painting sounds like the perfect job."

"And," Fred Wesley said, raising himself up, "I'm married."

"Whoa!"

"Christy Jo Bates."

Jonas stuck out his hand and they shook. "Congratulations. I remember Christy Jo. In the class just ahead of ours. How long's it been?"

"Two months."

"How's married life?"

"We argue some, but we always make up." He grinned.

"Making up, that's pretty good."

"I'm happy for you. And Christy Jo."

"We got a little house. You'll have to come see us. Christy Jo don't cook much, but she can make spaghetti."

"I'd like that."

"You looking for work, Jonas?"

"Not yet."

"Well, sometimes me and Rayfield need an extra hand."

Jonas held up his hand with the missing fingers. Fred Wesley gave it the once-over and then said, "Heck, that don't matter. Rayfield ain't got one of his thumbs, and he does okay."

"I'll think about it. Would you give me your best recommendation?"

Fred Wesley nodded solemnly. "You betcha. Well, I gotta go. Meeting Rayfield at Old Lady Benefield's house. We're doing exterior today. You have to think more when you're painting exterior or you might fall off the ladder." Fred Wesley gave him another hug. "I'll see you around."

"Fred Wesley," Jonas said, "Don't tell anybody else I'm here."

"Why not?"

"I just need a little time. Be quiet, get things squared away."

"Sure, Jonas. Ain't no harm in taking a little time." Then he bounded back to the truck, and just before he closed the door, he leaned out and yelled back to Jonas, "Remember, I may be slow, but I ain't stupid." Then he waved and was gone.

The rest of the way back to Doc's house, he thought about Fred Wesley, about how he was one of the best parts of the Copernicus he had known in the former life that seemed such old history. And the one part he had seen since he got back that didn't seem off-kilter and out of sorts.

Fred Wesley was Mayor Fleetwood Satterfield's son, born with a condition that made his brain a bit slower than others. In school, he was at the bottom of the class. Mayor Satterfield had told the teachers not to cut him any slack, and they didn't. But he attacked his books with grim determination and always managed to squeak by. He was quiet and didn't draw attention to himself, and the other kids pretty much ignored him, but Jonas was drawn to him because Fred Wesley seemed to be perfectly okay with himself.

What cemented it was the thing with Cody Reighard in the cafeteria. It was just Jonas and Fred Wesley at the table. Jonas finished first, picked up his tray, and left Fred Wesley diddling over his chocolate pudding. Jonas put his tray on the conveyor belt, silverware in the dishpan, and then turned to see Cody bending over Fred Wesley's back, mouth close to his ear, and reaching across his shoulders to pick up the chocolate pudding. Whatever Cody was whispering into Fred Wesley's ear was making him collapse into himself. Cody was now eating Fred Wesley's pudding, still talking. Jonas turned back to the conveyor, picked up his tray just before it disappeared, and walked back to the table. Cody, with his back to Jonas, never saw him coming. Holding the tray high, bashing Cody over the head with it. Cody went down in a yelping heap. Chocolate pudding flew. A teacher was on them like a banshee before it went any further.

They all went to the principal's office. Rodney was there, because Cody Reighard was a good first baseman. Rodney and Cody and the principal yammered at Jonas for awhile, and then Fred Wesley said, "Y'all shut up." They all stared in amazement. "Cody was screwing with me and Jonas stuck up for me. And that's the way it happened. I know when somebody's screwing with me, and I know who my friend is. I'm slow, but I ain't stupid."

By the time it was over, Cody apologized to Fred Wesley and Jonas apologized to Cody and Jonas got a one-day suspension, but Cody didn't because they had a game tomorrow. And they all got a stern talking-to, but the principal was easy on Fred Wesley, maybe partly because he was the mayor's son.

Fred Wesley was waiting outside when the last bell rang. "Jonas," he said, "you're skinny and he's a hunk. He coulda killed you. Why did you do that?"

Jonas smiled. "I'm slow, but I ain't stupid."

And they were friends.

And now, Jonas thought, Fred Wesley was real. Fred Wesley had hugged him and taken him to a place and time where a ghost can't go.

Breakfast. Pancakes from Miranda's special recipe that had some extra whole grain stuff and blueberries and craisins. Miranda fussed over him. "You're too skinny," she said. "In that hospital, didn't they feed you?"

"Not like you," he said. "Nobody's ever fed me like you."

In the couple of months he had spent at Doc's after Rodney threw him out, before he left for the Navy, he had actually gained a little weight. "It's good to have somebody in the house who likes to eat," she said with a scowl at Doc, who never cleaned his plate.

"But I have many fine qualities," Doc said. "I'm just trying to remember what they are."

"If you remember, you tell me," Miranda said, "then I tell all those other people who want to know."

Miranda and her husband Rafael had come from Mexico years ago, Rafael for work at Copernicus Manufacturing. When that closed, he started a landscaping and lawn care business, now ran three crews — but was, she said, thinking about cutting back. He had problems with his knees and Doc had told him they would have to be replaced before long. They were U.S. citizens, had raised four children and sent them into the world, two with college degrees. Miranda had been seeing after Doc Ainsley since the beginning, through Evelyn's cancer and death. After Evelyn died, Doc left for a year in Mexico, seeing about folks in the village where Miranda and Rafael had grown up. He needed something well away from death in Copernicus and the village needed a doctor. Miranda had come to the house every day to keep things ship-shape until he returned and opened his practice again. She and Doc were about the same age and seemed to Jonas almost like an old married couple, grousing at each other, especially when Doc didn't pick up his socks and underwear. Grousing in a way Doc and Evelyn would never have done. Evelyn was elegant, proper, reserved. Not the grousing kind.

"Miranda," Doc said, "go do the laundry. Or something."

Instead, Miranda shoveled two more pancakes onto Jonas's plate, made a good deal of noise at the sink until Jonas had finished them, and then marched out in a huff. They could hear her at work in the laundry room.

"What would you do if she got mad and left?" Jonas asked.

"Probably just croak," Doc said. They sat there for a while, finishing coffee. Then Doc said, "What are you gonna do?"

It took Jonas a moment. "You mean right now, or with the rest of my life?"

"Both, either."

"I don't know. I haven't thought much about it."

"You could, I suppose, just laze around here and vegetate. Right now, or for the rest of your life."

Jonas shrugged. "Do I have to decide?"

"Sooner or later. Or maybe not. Vegetating implies a certain amount of not deciding."

Jonas got up and took his dishes to the sink. He stood there for a moment, looking out at the back yard with its azalea bushes about to bloom and the Adirondack chairs in a semi-circle next to the koi pond. Rafael kept the place neat — shrubbery trimmed, grass mowed. Miranda fed the koi.

He felt Doc's eyes on him, turned back. "I went for a walk early," he said.

"I heard you leave."

"I walked all the way to the other end of town, and when I was on the way back, I saw Fred Wesley." He hesitated, trying to find words. "It all seemed so long ago, Doc. It's like I went off and lived somebody else's life, and now that I'm back, I don't know whose life I'm living. The whole place looks different. Smaller, like it's been squeezed together or something. Has it changed that much?"

"Like your room."

"Yeah."

"I don't think so. Not much changes in Copernicus, not over three years. But I can understand how it might seem that way to you."

"And Fred Wesley. He was my best friend, and I've gone three years without even as much as sending a postcard. Now he's married and got a job and living his own life. And I'm guessing a lot of other people, ones I was in school with, have moved on. But me..."

Doc nodded.

"I don't see how I can stay, Doc."

"If not here, where?"

Jonas raised his arms in frustration. "I don't know. I really don't know."

"Jonas," Doc said, "you've been to a foreign country, and I don't just mean Afghanistan."

Jonas ducked his head. "Yeah. And it's like part of me is still there. Like I lost me."

Doc stood and crossed to the sink and put an arm over Jonas's shoulder. They stood there like that for a moment and then Doc said, "Where do you think you might find yourself, Jonas?"

"I don't know."

"Somewhere out yonder?"

"Maybe."

"Or maybe here, where there are people who know you. Who love you. Including me."

Jonas felt something small but significant break somewhere inside. It took awhile before he could speak and then he said, "I love you too, Doc. But all the rest? I just don't know."

"Okay. One part of me says take your time. But another part says, *do* something. It may not be exactly the right thing, but do something to move off square one. I'm not much of a fan of vegetating."

"What, then?"

"Two things I want you to do today. First, get on the phone and call over to the VA hospital and make an appointment. Will you do that?"

"I guess."

"I'll take that as a yes."

"And then?"

"Go see your mother."

Jonas froze. "I can't…"

"Damn right you can," Doc said. "That was a shitty thing you did, Jonas, freezing her out."

"I didn't…well, not *her*."

"What did you think? You could punish Rodney and not punish her? Think of what she's gone through the past three years with you gone, especially the way you left without a word and never got in touch, worrying about you, and then now with what's happened. She's your mother."

Jonas turned with a jerk, pushing Doc's arm aside. "Dad threw me out, Doc. And I swore I'd never go back in his house, not ever."

"He's not there," Doc said.

"What?"

"Go ask Gladys."

FOUR

She hugged him and cried.

And he felt like a shit.

"I'm sorry," he said when she finally let him go.

"It's all right," she said, holding his face in her hands. "Everything's all right. You're home."

Everything wasn't all right, of course, and whatever home had been, it wasn't that any more. But still, he could feel some of the hard thing at his core ease just a bit. He didn't want to punish anybody. Doc was right about that.

They sat together on the couch in the living room and she held onto both his hands with both of hers. "Tell me how you are," she said.

"Pretty much okay. Everything's healing. I'm gonna be fine. No permanent damage."

"That's what Frank said."

"He checked me over." He tried to manage a smile. "Nothing missing…except…" he held up his left hand.

She clutched his hand and touched the place where the fingers had been and was silent for a long time. Finally she said, "Where are you going to put your wedding ring?"

"If I ever get married, maybe I'll just wear it on a chain around my neck."

They both laughed and that eased things a lot. She put his hand back in his lap and started to rise. "I'm making some fresh iced tea."

"Doc said Dad isn't here."

She sat back and stared at her own hands for a moment and he thought again, as he had all the way over here, *Did she finally get fed up with the sonofabitch and kick him out? Finally?*

"Rodney's had a stroke," she said.

"What? When?"

"Two months ago. He was in the hospital for awhile and now he's in rehabilitation. He almost died. But he didn't."

"And?"

"He's paralyzed on his left side and his speech is affected."

Jonas took a deep breath, tried to make some sense of the stuff in his head coming from all directions — Rodney, pain, guilt, anger, disappointment, Gladys. "I'm sorry," he said, though it didn't come close, if anything could. Then he thought, *two months ago. Right after the last time they tried to see me at the hospital. Did I...* Then, "Is he gonna recover?"

"He's made some progress." She hesitated. "I'm bringing him home next week."

"Mom, you can't handle..."

"I'll have help. Home health care, physical therapist. And..."

She fell silent and it took him a moment to realize. "Oh. Mom...no."

Her face fell and she looked ready to cry again, but then suddenly she brightened and gave him a smile and patted his wounded hand. "You've got your own life, honey. You're a grown man now. Not my little boy any more." He started to speak, searching for words, but she shushed him with her fingers on his lips. "Not another word about it."

"Don't do that," he said, more sharply than he intended. "You always try to brush things off, pretend it doesn't matter, make like everything's okay. Well, it's not okay. Look, I'll help if I can, but I can't come back here."

She stood. "I'll bring the iced tea to the patio."

He wandered around the back yard while he waited. She was taking her time — maybe, he thought, convincing herself, as she had so often done, that things really were okay. Despite everything. The thought of it filled him with sadness.

Sweet, quiet, uncomplaining Gladys. Twenty years taking direction from a grumpy asshole that Jonas couldn't ever remember her standing up to. When it was just the two of them, especially after

Byrd left to play football at Auburn, she comforted and soothed him. But when Rodney got on one of his tirades, she would say, "Just ignore it." Ignore? When Rodney could cut him into little pieces with a word or a look? When he tried so hard to get Rodney to approve of at least one little thing about him, and always failed? Okay, he wasn't an athlete, he wasn't the smartest kid in his class, he was skinny, his voice was a half-octave higher than most of the other boys his age. But wasn't there something? Anything? Gladys told him over and over that she loved him, that he had — her favorite phrase — *many fine qualities*. But go to bat for him with Rodney? No. He loved her, and that seemed at times the only solid thing he could lay claim to. But along with the love was the hurt and resentment. *She never has my back.*

Or, she would say, "We don't want to get him upset." *We.* So he tried very hard not to because he understood that it was a way he could protect her, make things a little easier. It had taken awhile, leaving home, joining the Navy, going in harm's way, to understand that at his core he had become — really, had always been — a caregiver.

So now? He didn't even know if he could take care of himself. The only thing he knew for sure right now was that being a caregiver had nearly gotten him killed. The mere thought of taking care of Rodney Boulware felt like another kind of death.

He forced himself to get outside his own head. The yard was in poor shape. There was once, Gladys had told him, a formal garden here. Her father, the Copernicus Manufacturing guy, had bought two hundred acres on the north edge of town, carved out a sizable chunk for his own brick-and-white-columns home, and surrounded it with all manner of growing things. The rest of the land, he turned into Copernicus Country Club and nice houses. His house sat on a knoll, and from any side, you could see the golf course spreading out below, fairways and greens and tee boxes. No bunkers, because the old man hated playing out of sand. Years later, when Rodney came along, he tore out most of the garden stuff. Too much trouble, he said. Now, what shrubbery was left needed trimming, the grass was ragged, and the house needed a coat of trim paint. And now, there were bunkers. The old man would have been mortified.

Gladys appeared with a tray — crystal pitcher, glasses with

ice, plate of cookies — balancing it carefully with one hand as she closed the back door. She brought it to the patio and set it down on a low table that needed a coat of rust arrester and paint.

"I'll get Pee Wee," she said, and went back in the house.

She was back in a couple of minutes with a dog, a small white fur ball, eyes barely visible behind a shag of hair. Jonas was speechless. Rodney hated dogs. She sat, Pee Wee in her lap. "Don't you think he's cute?" she asked as she reached across Pee Wee and poured the tea.

"I didn't hear him in there. Wouldn't he bark or something?"

"He's deaf."

"Oh."

"He's been so much company."

"Is he house trained?"

"Of course," she said. "He's not a puppy, he's two years old. Fleetwood and Mildred had him, but Mildred finally figured out that she was allergic."

Jonas took a big drink of tea. "He's no bigger than a fart," he said without thinking.

"Jonas, please."

"Well, he isn't."

"Did the Navy teach you nasty speech?"

"No, the Marine Corps."

"Well, I'd appreciate it if you would leave it with the Marine Corps."

"Okay."

Pee Wee sat quietly in her lap. Jonas couldn't tell whether the dog was looking at him or not. Maybe, behind that shag of hair, he was also blind. Gladys sipped tea with one hand and petted Pee Wee with the other. Jonas didn't say anything for awhile, and neither did Gladys, and then she started chattering about her charity work. For as long as Jonas could remember, Gladys had been up to her eyeballs in charity. Red Cross blood drive, tutoring at the elementary school, packing gift boxes for Samaritan's Purse, honchoing the library's used book sale. She was pretty much into everything at the Presbyterian Church that needed a volunteer, and if there wasn't enough of that, she helped out at the Baptist and the Methodist and the Lutheran. Here in the late Spring, she said, things were winding down a bit, and that was good because she went every day to the rehab place in Waylonsville to see about Rodney.

Jonas contributed an occasional nod or "Uh-huh" and thought about the moment in high school when he realized Gladys was doing penance, as if a tsunami of good deeds could somehow atone for the disaster that had been Copernicus Manufacturing. They were in church at First Presbyterian, singing, "Gladly The Cross I'd Bear." He looked over at Gladys and could almost imagine her dragging a cross along Main Street.

He was lost in thought when she asked, "Did you hear what I said?"

"Huh?"

"What are people going to think, you back home and living over there with Frank when you have a perfectly good…"

"Mom," he said, "I'm not living here. It was okay for me to live at Doc's for two months when Dad threw me out, and everybody in town knew that."

"That's different."

"No it's not. Everybody in town knew that Dad punched me out in front of a lot of people on the golf course and then ran me off. And that you let him." He realized he was close to shouting now, but he couldn't help it.

Gladys didn't blink an eye. Jonas stared at her, trying to calm himself, and thinking there had always been this hidden part of her that you couldn't reach. Her mask. In his childhood, she might comfort and soothe, but there was never the feeling that she truly gave herself.

"I had no choice," she said now.

"What do you mean, you had no choice?"

"It's not anything you would understand."

"Try me."

"No."

He stood. "Back there when you let Dad kick me out, Doc took me in. And this time, when I was in a really bad place, he came and got me again. So if I've got a home right now, it's at Doc's."

She sat there for a moment looking down at the dog, rubbing his back. And finally she said, "Well, all right."

"Mom, have you told anybody I'm back?"

"Of course not. You living over there…"

"Well, don't. I've got to go. Thanks for the iced tea."

She pursed her lips and looked up at him. "I want you to build me a wheelchair ramp."

* * * * *

There was something in the bed with him. He could feel its presence, and then he reached and touched and recoiled in horror at the feel of flesh, hair, blood. Lieutenant Hammer's head. He yelled, toppled from the bed, slithered backward on his bare ass to the far wall and huddled there. And then the wall behind him collapsed into rubble. He screamed, "Hammer, you sonofabitch!"

"Jonas!" The voice from somewhere at a great distance. And then Doc.

They sat by the koi pond as light began to faintly shade the east. Doc had made coffee. They drank in silence, deep in the Adirondacks. In the pond, the koi were mottled shadows of themselves. Jonas could feel himself down there in the gray water with them — quiet, hiding among the weeds, watching them dip and swirl. He was very still, afraid of breaking apart and spilling what he was so carefully holding inside, polluting the pond, killing the koi. *I never, never again want to be part of anything that's dying.*

They stayed that way for a long time before Jonas rose from the depths of the pond and sat again in the chair, the coffee cold in his cup. "I don't know what to do," he said finally, letting go of it.

Doc waited awhile longer before he set his cup on the broad armrest of the chair and said, "Whatever you do, I don't think you can do it on your own. Or should even try."

"It's all mixed up together. Mom, Dad, the war…"

Doc waited, brow furrowed, before he said, "I've always thought we all carry a sack slung over our shoulders. Everything that's ever happened to us, everything we've *thought* about what's happened to us, it goes in that sack. Good stuff, bad stuff, stuff that's neither. All in there, all jumbled up together, and the longer we live, the more stuff."

"Yeah. And it gets pretty goddamn heavy."

"You've got a pretty heavy sack because you've lived a lot to be as young as you are."

"Sometimes," Jonas said, "I feel like a fucking old man."

"Like me."

Jonas turned to look at Doc, the light strong enough now that he could see the curves, the lines, the furrows of Doc's weathered face. "I guess you've got a lot of shit in your sack, too. Eve...Mrs. Ainsley, being a doctor, all that."

"Uh-huh."

"So that's it? You just tote the goddamn sack around with you all your life?"

"Lots of people do. It makes 'em stoop under the weight, and sometimes stumble, and they might have only the vaguest notion of why."

"Lots of people."

"But some folks stop every once in awhile, put the sack down, open it up, rummage around, get a good look at what's there, maybe rearrange things so that it's easier to carry."

"But," Jonas said, "the stuff never goes away."

"Not really. But the load shifts a little. And maybe you learn to live with it."

Jonas let out a long sigh. "So that's me?"

"If you're willing. I think it's probably not easy to look inside your particular sack. Lots of stuff to deal with, some of it downright wretched. But the alternative..."

"Some..." Jonas waited for awhile before he let it out, "...give up."

"Jonas, have you ever thought about giving up?"

"No, Doc. Honestly. I think about Sergeant Willis, so fucked up in the head that he didn't see any other way out. And I think, that's not me. But that doesn't mean I'm not fucked up some myself."

"There's another way you can try to deal with it."

"What?"

"Self medicating. Alcohol, drugs, so forth. Are you doing any of that?"

"I've thought about it," Jonas said.

"It's a dead end, and I mean that literally. It might help

for awhile, but then it just becomes another big piece of shit in that sack you tote around. From what I read and see and hear, when you figure out that stuff is just making things worse, that's when the giving up starts. That's a bad piece of road that leads to the edge of nowhere."

Jonas thought about it for a moment. "I guess I'm afraid if I got into that stuff, it might take me where I don't want to go. Remembering, you know. Being more fucked up than I already am."

"Then you've got to do something about being fucked up."

Jonas started to speak, but then it hit him, a blow in the soul — the realization of just how incredibly miserable he was, and fragile, and wretchedly sad and the whole fucking screaming mess. He started to cry and didn't make even the slightest effort to stop, the poison leaking out. Doc eased himself out of his chair and came to Jonas's and lifted him up and held him tightly until the misery subsided a little.

"Help me," he whispered.

FIVE

Miranda came and fixed breakfast and they ate while she fussed over them. And then Jonas went upstairs and made up the bed where Hammer's head had been and settled into Doc's study with a book while Doc saw to Mayor Fleetwood Satterfield in his office downstairs. The Mayor had lost twenty-five pounds, but still complained about his hips.

At mid-morning, Doc came upstairs.

"Did you call the VA?"

"Actually, I did. They said they can see me in a couple of months."

"I figured that. Lots of vets are really pissed at the VA these days. But I've got a friend on the staff at the VA Hospital," he said. "I'll call him. If that's okay."

Jonas shrugged.

"Maybe he can speed things up."

"Okay."

"Now," said Doc, "get up off your ass and go see Lieu-tenant."

Lieutenant Wooley wasn't a lieutenant, not in the usual sense. That was just the name his mother gave him when he was born. "She thought about 'Captain,'" Lieutenant had told Jonas years before, "but she thought it might give me the big head. It drove 'em crazy when I was in the Army. None of the officers or sergeants would use my first name. The guys in my outfit thought it was funny as hell, and they would salute and call me 'sir' — not around any officers or sergeants, of course — and finally they just fell into calling me Wooley Booger."

Lieutenant had done a tour in Vietnam that he didn't talk

much about, saved some money, borrowed a little more when he came home, and bought a big cow pasture two miles out of town, which he turned into a driving range and a nine-hole par-three course. He carved it out himself on a tractor, planted grass, sodded greens, and when it was greened-in and in business, did all the maintenance. Took agronomy courses at a community college. Kept it in pristine condition.

In his youth, Lieutenant had caddied at Copernicus Country Club. Glady's father, who ran things, didn't want golf carts on his course. You could tote your own bag or get a caddy. Lieutenant studied the swings of the better players, then sneaked back at night with a sackful of balls he had found, and a few clubs the members had discarded, and tried to imitate what he had seen. He never told anybody, especially the other caddies. A black kid hanging around the white folks' country club after hours? It would get his ass fired, maybe worse.

After Lieutenant got his driving range and par-three the way he wanted them, he opened for business and advertised in the newspaper that lessons were available. Doc Ainsley was his first customer. He cured Doc's slice. Doc went back to Copernicus Country Club and told other members, who had slices and hooks and shanks of their own that had defied the ministrations of the club pro. Lieutenant cured some of them, too. He had an Airstream travel trailer which doubled as living quarters and pro shop, enough equipment to keep up the maintenance, and a growing reputation.

Jonas hadn't been there since the day before he left for the Navy. Now the Airstream had been replaced by a neat white frame building with a red metal roof. The Airstream was parked out back. Jonas peered through the screen door, opened it halfway, called in, "Captain Wooley?"

"Smartass," came from somewhere in a back room, then Lieutenant peered around a corner. "Hmmm," he said, "you look vaguely familiar. Close the door. You're letting the flies out," and disappeared.

It was a small, neat workshop where Lieutenant was bent over a bench, putting a new grip on a three-wood locked in a vise, intent on the work. Without looking up, he pointed to a bar stool in a corner, and Jonas pulled it over to the workbench and sat watching.

Through a window at the back of the bench he could see the range, where a half-dozen golfers were bashing balls. Beyond, he could see players on the par-three course. Off to the side, equipment parked under a long, low shed. That was new, too.

Lieutenant raised up from the bench, took the three-wood out of the vise, held it up and sighted down the length of it, grip to head. He gave a grunt of satisfaction and set it aside with a collection of other clubs that already had the new grips, all except for a driver, which he picked up. "Mack Woodie's third driver in a year. Just bought the damn thing, and he's already got me tinkering with it — new shaft, new grip. Mack's an equipment freak, always looking for the next piece of magic to make him a golfer. Hell, what Mack needs is to go out in his backyard and shoot himself in the right shoulder to make him stop coming over the top."

"Good to see you too," Jonas said.

Lieutenant stuck out his hand. "Been awhile."

They shook. "Yeah."

"Thought about you a lot."

"Same here."

Lieutenant looked him up and down. "Well, you're still the same scrawny little shit that used to come out here and make a nuisance of yourself."

Jonas smiled. He had learned early on that Lieutenant jawed at people he liked, and expected you to jaw back. "Can't believe I wasted all that time messing around at a place like this when I coulda been chasing girls and doing other useful stuff."

Lieutenant grunted with satisfaction. "What time is it?"

"Ten after five."

"You drink beer?"

Jonas thought about what Doc had said. "Sometimes. Not much."

There was a small shelter — open sides, tin roof — off to one side of the range. There were benches, but they carried a couple of lawn chairs and sat drinking cold Bud Lights. The first taste took him jarringly to Ray Willis's back yard, but he forced the thought away. *Don't go there.*

The range was crowded now, every hitting area occupied — kids, old farts, everything in between. He watched for awhile. Some godawful swings, some who knew what they were doing, some who seemed to have come to a measure of peace with their games, some who hadn't. Frustrated shake of shoulders, mutterings, looks of pained despair. "Golf," Doc had said to him once, "is either elegantly maddening or maddeningly elegant. I haven't figured out which. Maybe both." And he told him what Mark Twain had said about golf: *a good walk spoiled.*

"I can tell which ones are taking lessons," Jonas said.

"Hell, most of 'em are taking lessons. It's just that with a lot of 'em, the lessons ain't takin'."

It was a nice late afternoon — warm but not hot, a scattering of clouds, the *thwack* of struck balls. Jonas settled into the beer, felt himself easing a bit after last night and early this morning. Still raw in places, but easing. From the first time he came, age twelve, it had always made him feel better to be here, to spend time with Lieutenant, who judged nothing except his golf swing. And his ability to jaw back.

"Thank God and the legislature for daylight savings time," Lieutenant said. "Back in the sixties, when the legislature was considering it, the Farm Bureau was opposed. Some idiot got up before a committee and said, 'It will confuse the farm animals.' But they passed it anyway. Now," the hand with the beer bottle swept across the range, "I get 'em out here until past eight. Couple of months, past nine. And as far as I know, the farm animals are okay."

"Looks like you've done okay," Jonas said.

"Passable. Ain't getting' rich, but then affluence ain't all it's cracked up to be."

"All this new stuff…the building, equipment…"

"Well, I still ain't a Captain."

"That's good," Jonas said. "You'd make a terrible Captain."

They sat there finishing their beers, watching the golfers, and then Lieutenant took the empties and went back to the pro shop and got two more. While he was gone, Jonas noticed the tall, skinny kid down at the end of the range. Long, unruly hair, baggy shorts and a faded yellow shirt. He was hacking away, one ball followed quickly by another, by another. An incredibly long, ungainly back-swing that wrapped the club behind his shoulders, then a savage unwinding that somehow, just as incredibly, got the club-face somewhere in the neighborhood of the ball. He made contact every time, but the results were all over the lot — a banana slice one moment, a wicked snap hook the next, and once in awhile, something distant, high, elegant. He was like a long, thin spring, coiling and uncoiling, his whole body flailing away, fighting itself. Jonas stared, and then he thought, *Angry. At golf, or something else?* And then he thought…

"Who is the kid?" he asked when Lieutenant was back. "He looks…I don't know, kind of familiar."

"Ben. Cameron. No reason you'd know him."

He watched the kid for another minute. Something in the way he moved, maybe? Set of his jaw, the way he gave a frustrated shake of his head, hair flying, when he mis-hit. "He looks so pissed."

"He comes out here a couple of days a week. I let him run the ball retriever, pick up the range, then give him a couple of baskets to practice. Some days he looks like he's got talent. Others, well…"

"Are you teaching him?"

"He don't want lessons, just range balls. He's pretty closed off. Keeps to himself. Always down at the far end of the range."

"That back-swing…it's a wonder he doesn't crack a rib."

"No shit." Lieutenant gave him a long look. "You know from back-swings."

"Well," Jonas said, "used to."

"What I hear," Lieutenant went on, "he's got a pretty screwed-up situation at home. His mom's a bad piece — booze, drugs, men in and out. When she's not fucked up, she cleans houses. The kid's father — if she ever knew who it was — long gone. So I guess he comes out here and takes it out on golf balls." Lieutenant took a long pull on the beer. "Like somebody else I know."

"Yeah," Jonas said. "Like somebody else." He waited a long moment before he said, "I don't know what I woulda done without this."

"Probably chased girls and done other useful stuff."

"Uh-huh."

"Did I ever tell you how I learned to play golf?" Lieutenant asked.

"Well, you told me about caddying and all."

"Vietnam," Lieutenant said.

"There was a golf course in Vietnam?"

"Not so much as a putt-putt. But in some kind of rear eche-lon fuck-up, somebody sent a set of clubs and several hundred Titleist balls to where we were. Left-handed clubs. And I'm right-handed. But there was this other guy who was a lefty and a scratch golfer, and he gave lessons as long as the balls held out. We were on a low hill, and you could see the rice paddies stretching out toward the Mekong. We took some stakes and painted 'em orange, and when we went out on patrol we'd hammer 'em in the ground. A hundred yards, one-fif-ty, two hundred, two-fifty. By the time the balls ran out, I could hit a driver past the two hundred and could land a nine iron within ten yards of the one-fifty. Left-handed. The other guy, he was dead on every time. Helluva ball striker. But then he stepped on a mine."

"Shit," Jonas said.

"Yeah. When we rotated back to the States, I kept it up. And then I got out and came home. And did this."

"Do you think about him?"

"Every time I hit a golf ball."

There was nothing else to say about that, so they sat there and worked on their beers for awhile longer. Finally, Lieutenant turned and put a hand on Jonas's shoulder. "I need some help out here. I'm getting old and creaky. Hell, I can hardly hit a drive two-twenty-five any more."

Jonas looked at Lieutenant, then away. "I may not stay."

"May not?"

"I'm trying to work it all out. Got some stuff I need to deal with."

"I understand." And the way he said it, Jonas thought, he maybe did understand. Probably talked to Doc some. Knew pretty much what was in the peddler's sack Jonas toted around, the old stuff and some of the new. And then, there was Vietnam.

"There's a lot more to a place like this than just golf," Lieu-tenant said. "There's the business part, and if you don't figure that out, the golf goes away like a fart in the wind. What to buy, what to sell, what to charge, all that stuff. I had to figure it out the hard way. But I could teach it to you. And one of these days…"

"I quit," Jonas blurted.

"I know you did, and I know why you did, Jonas."

Of course he did, Jonas thought. They had never talked

about it, about how he tossed aside his golf clubs and walked off the seventh green at the state tournament, about how Rodney had fucked up golf for him. Lieutenant had never said a word about it after it happened, but he knew. Hell, everybody in town knew. "I haven't picked up a club in more than three years."

"I figured that."

Jonas finished his beer and handed the bottle to Lieutenant. "I guess I oughta go."

"Think about it. While you're sorting stuff out."

"Okay."

Jonas was several yards away when he turned and walked back. He held up his left hand. "Besides, there's this. Could you do anything about this?"

"No, but you could. If you wanted."

* * * * *

When Jonas was twelve, Doc Ainsley called him one day while Rodney was at baseball practice and said, "I'm picking you up in fifteen minutes. Wear shorts and a shirt with a collar." He had a new set of junior golf clubs in his car and he took Jonas to Lieutenant's range. "This man," he said to Jonas, "is the closest thing I know to a golf guru. He cured my slice, and that, in my book, makes him a guru. Do what he says." He looked Jonas' skinny frame up and down. "I think it might be your sport." Doc left him there while he went to the country club, where he was one of the pretty fair golfers.

For the next two years, Jonas learned. Once a week, Doc would pick him up at home after school and take him to Lieutenant's. They would spend a half-hour working together, then Jonas would hit range balls until Doc came back. He learned the game from the bottom — putt, chip, wedge, irons. Three months after they started, Jonas was on the range one afternoon doing his stretches (Lieutenant insisted on ten minutes of stretches before picking up a club. "You may be a limber-back now, but one of these days you'll be a stove-up old fart. So get in the habit.") when Lieutenant walked over from the Airstream. He waited while Jonas finished, and then, when Jonas reached for the pitching wedge in his bag, Lieutenant said, "No. This one." And he pulled out the driver.

Jeezus. The big stick.

Lieutenant handed the club to Jonas, who stood there holding it awkwardly, then looked up, questioning. "Same grip, same swing. Keep it smooth." He put his hands together, swung with his shoulders. "Tick-tock." He handed Jonas a ball and a tee. Lieutenant stopped him when he started to tee it up. "What's your target? Never step up to a golf ball unless you mean it, and you don't mean it if you don't know what your target is." Jonas pointed to a flag about a hundred yards out. "That's a pussy target," Lieutenant said, "but at least it's a target. Now get your alignment, tee the ball closer to your front foot, stance a little wider." Jonas set himself, then looked up at him again. "Well, what are you waiting for? Knock the piss out of it."

Jonas' heart was in his throat. He felt like he might wet his pants. But he took a deep breath, made his hands and forearms soft like Lieutenant had taught him, and felt himself easing into the mind-set they had worked on over and over. *Just me and the ball.* Then he knocked the piss out of the golf ball. They watched it fly straight and true, right over the top of the target flag but going way past, gaining altitude until it reached an apex and came to earth, took two bounces, and settled.

"Sonofabitch," Lieutenant said softly.

Jonas turned to him in alarm. "What did I do wrong?"

Lieutenant grunted. "That was a good 'sonofabitch,' not a bad 'sonofabitch.'"

"It was okay?"

"Uh-huh." He took the driver from Jonas, took his time wiping the club head with a towel, slipping the cover back on, sticking it back in the bag. He turned back to Jonas and stood there for a moment, maybe searching for the right words. Finally: "What you did to that golf ball just now, you can't teach that. It's either there or it ain't. It's there. But don't get the big head, or I'll have to start calling you Captain."

Jonas laughed, feeling so good he thought he might need to run all the way home.

"What do you feel when you swing a club and hit a ball?" Lieutenant asked.

Now it was Jonas' turn to search for words. "Like...I'm free or something."

Lieutenant nodded. "That's good. Because you gotta play free if you're gonna do what I think you can do. Golf will drive you nuts if you let it, if you try to play from up here," he tapped Jonas's head, "so you've got to be in charge, and that comes from way down in here." He tapped his gut.

Jonas looked at the bag, the driver. "Can I do it again?"

"Not today. Go home and think about it. Just play that shot over and over in your mind. Enjoy the hell out of it. You had an orgasm yet?"

"A what?"

"Never mind. You will. And when you do, think about how you felt when you hit that shot just now. It will come in a close second to the orgasm."

At the dinner table a week later. Jonas had fine-tuned his ability to read signals, and he could tell something wasn't right. Rodney was quiet, but pleasant. Rodney didn't do pleasant well. Jonas watched and waited, and when they were finished, Rodney wiped his mouth with his napkin, set it aside, and looked at Jonas. "I was at the barber shop today," he said, "and some of the guys were talking about how you've been out at that run-down driving range hitting golf balls."

Jonas took in air. "Yes sir."

"You want to learn to play golf, you go to Tommy at the club. I've set you up with a lesson right after school tomorrow."

Jonas felt a pit opening up under his chair. Tommy was an idiot, everybody knew that, but he stayed on at the club by kissing the members' rear ends. Doc Ainsley said he had taken a lesson from Tommy, hoping to cure his slice. After an hour of pounding balls and getting nowhere, he had turned to Tommy and asked, "Why am I doing that?" Tommy scratched his head, then his balls, and said, "I don't rightly know." And then Doc had gone to Lieutenant and been healed. A guru.

Jonas stared at his plate, feeling Rodney's eyes boring in on him. He knew better than to look at Gladys, down at the other end of the table. No help there. He started to speak, but the words stuck in his throat. He swallowed hard. And then he said, "No sir."

It hung there in the air, naked and trembling, for a long time.

"What did you just say to me?"

"I said, 'No sir.'"

He caught a movement out of the corner of his eye and looked up with a jerk to see Rodney's hand raised, making a fist. "I will knock you through that goddamned wall," he bellowed.

Jonas sat up straight, squared his shoulders, turned toward Rodney, looked him in the eye. *Go ahead, you bastard. For once, just go ahead and do it.* Rodney's fist started toward him but Gladys stopped it in mid-air with a sharp cry. "No!" Rodney's head jerked around to glare open-mouthed at her. "Frank Ainsley is taking him to the driving range."

Rodney seemed to swell up into something Jonas had never seen before — something beastly, terrible, hateful, but also something else...*woundedness?* He leapt to his feet, his chair crashing to the floor. He picked up his glass of iced tea and flung it against a wall where it smashed into a hundred pieces. Then he left. Jonas waited for a minute or so until he heard the back door slam, then fetched a towel and cleaned up the mess. When he finished he turned finally to look at Gladys, saw that she was slumped onto the table, shoulders shaking with silent sobs. Jonas knelt beside her chair and put his arm around her, comforting her from whatever terrible thing had just happened. He didn't ask, just comforted.

It was two weeks before Rodney said a word to either of them. Gladys slept on the couch. Jonas gave him a wide berth. But he kept going to Lieutenant.

* * * * *

They sat again in the evening by the koi pond, Doc with a neat Scotch and Jonas with his thoughts. Doc waited for him.

"Lieutenant offered me a job," Jonas said after awhile.

"I thought he might."

"I don't think I could work out there."

"You know how much Lieutenant thinks of you."

"Yeah. And me him. But I don't think I'll want to do golf again."

"Ever?"

"Probably."

"Then something else?"

"I don't know."

Doc held up his glass to the fading light, swirled the Scotch around, then took another sip. Doc could make a neat Scotch last for a long time, as long as you needed.

"Tell me about Dad," Jonas said.

"Rodney almost died," Doc said. "He's in pretty bad shape."

"Is he gonna get better?"

"With a stroke, you can generally figure on the chance for improvement for up to a year."

Jonas shook his head. "I sound like a wretched sonofabitch when I say this, but I don't care if he does or not."

"Yes, you sound like a wretched sonofabitch, Jonas, but if that's the way you feel…"

"I've been thinking all day about Mom."

"And?"

"I can't live over there, I get sick at my stomach even thinking about being around the place. And with Mom…there's all this junk going around in my head. It makes me want to crawl in a hole. She never…"

"You don't know *never*, Jonas," Doc interrupted. "You don't know what she did, what she said, to make things a little easier for you. You know the times she didn't interfere, but you don't know the times she did."

"You do?"

"Some," he said. Then, "There's a very great deal you don't know."

"What?"

"That's between you and your mother, and you'll have to work it out. If you want to, that is. But I will say this, Jonas, you can't go on being a wounded child forever. What you've got to deal with, the mess in your soul you brought back from over there, a child can't handle it. And I don't think you can do it out on the road some-where."

They sat in silence as night came on and the koi disappeared beneath the blackness of the water and a slight breeze rustled the tops

Villages

of the trees that sheltered the yard.

Finally, Jonas said, "Then I guess I'll have to stay for awhile."

SIX

He dreamed of the platoon, or at least what he supposed must be the platoon. They were nothing more than wispy figures at the edge of his consciousness, ghost shapes in tones of gray. They stood back in a cluster, so close together it was hard to tell where one ended and the next began. Then he understood that they were waiting. He raised his hand but there was no response. Maybe, he thought, I'm invisible. And then one of them stepped away from the rest and took a few steps toward him and he realized after a moment it was Ray Willis. Then the ground began to open below Ray and Ray looked down and saw what was happening and he stretched out his arms toward Jonas. But Jonas was trapped — outside himself, but inside whoever it was he had lost. He struggled, but he couldn't find himself and the gap in the earth widened and Ray began to slip into it and Jonas cried with the frustration of failure.

He woke, bathed in sweat, thrashing against the sheets. He got up and took another pill and eventually sleep returned, but there wasn't much to it.

They ate mostly in silence, and when they were finished Doc took the breakfast dishes and silverware to the sink. At the far end of the house, they could hear Miranda's vacuum cleaner. Doc came back and sat across from Jonas. His lips moved, but nothing came out, and Jonas thought there had been several times in the past couple of weeks when Doc seemed on the verge of something, but backed away. Instead, he reached across the table, placed a cool hand on Jonas's forehead, brushed back the hair. "You need a haircut."

Jonas nodded.

"Rough night?"

Another nod.

"Want to talk about it?"

Jonas clasped his hands on the table top and stared at them. "It was Sergeant Willis. He wanted me to save him, but..."

"You couldn't."

"He blew his brains out."

"I know. The police in Jacksonville said you were perfectly calm when they got there, answered all their questions. A suicide, nothing to do with you. So they let you go, and you left, and that's when you came apart."

"But it *was*...to do with me." And then the words came pouring out, everything he could remember about Ray Willis — the war, the way he took care of his Marines, Juliette, the way Ray's soul seemed to have come off with his foot. And then he told what Ray had said to him just before he put the .45 to his temple.

Doc listened without interrupting, and then when Jonas finished and looked up, he could see a sheen in Doc's eyes. "That was," he said gently, "an unspeakable thing to do, trying to pull you down into his hellhole. You understand that, don't you?"

"I don't know."

Doc sat back in his chair, took a moment to compose himself. "I can't begin to imagine what you've been through. You've always been pretty buttoned down, kept your own counsel, tended your own fire, and I know where that came from. A way of coping. But now, it's a lot more than that. I see a young man..." he paused, on the verge again, then, "...I like a lot who's shut off from himself and who's aging before my eyes, and it breaks my heart. That, and knowing I'm powerless to help."

"You've helped a lot. Being here..."

"But it's not enough. I'm just an old country sawbones. You need somebody who understands what you're going through and can help you figure out how to deal with it. Whatever happened over there..."

"But I don't know what happened, Doc. At the hospital, they kept trying to make me remember. But I can't."

"But you remember your Sergeant Willis and what kind of madness that turned out to be, and maybe that's connected to what happened in Afghanistan. So that's the elephant in your room, what you can't remember."

"I guess."

"I'm hoping to hear from my contact at the VA Hospital today."

"I don't know, Doc."

"What did they tell you at Bethesda…about dealing with your situation."

Jonas sighed. "They said it's pay me now or pay me later."

"Well," Doc said, "it's later."

He went upstairs, showered, dressed, looked at himself in the mirror. Doc was right, he needed a haircut. Long enough that it covered his ears and was beginning to curl up in the back. But the thought of going to a barber shop — people, conversation, questions — he couldn't do that. He needed a shave, too. A week's scraggle of light brown fuzz along his jawline. Doc had brought him a razor and shaving gel last week and he had managed to scrape off what was there, but the feel of blade across skin made him nauseated.

He found Doc at his desk downstairs, toying idly with a ball-point, turning it end over end, staring out the window at the morning. Doc looked up, put the pen down. Jonas stood in the doorway for a moment, then: "Doc, do you fail?"

Doc pursed his lips. "In what sense, Jonas?"

"With people. Your patients. You know, you try as hard as you can, but…"

Doc ran his hand along his skull, the thinning white hair, closed his eyes. Seconds went by. Jonas felt a pang of guilt. Maybe something that pained Doc so much he… But then Doc opened his eyes and looked directly into Jonas's, locking in on him. "Medicine is an act of failure. If you succeeded, in the ultimate sense of the word, you would keep everybody healthy and alive forever. But you don't, you can't. A disease you can't do anything about, terrible habits that people won't give up, accidents, wearing-out in old age. War."

He took Jonas by the arm. "Let's go sit out on the front porch."

When they were settled, Doc pointed down the street to a neat frame one-story, painted a dark green, with a big pecan tree in the front yard.

"That house down there…well, I'll tell you about failure, the first time it tore my guts out. Years ago, not long after I opened my practice, fresh out of residency and cocky as hell about healing the world. A kid named Francis, eight years old. Playing on the sidewalk while his dad mowed the lawn. The blade hit something, part of it came off, ripped into Francis's chest." Doc stopped, took a breath, his face twisted with old hurt. Jonas felt himself recoil. *Don't go there!* But Doc went on. "His dad picked him up and ran over here. Blood everywhere, pulse almost non-existent. I brought him back once, but then..." Doc looked away, then down at the floor.

"God..." Jonas whispered.

It was a long moment before Doc looked up again. "Evelyn and I couldn't have children. We were thinking about adoption. But after that kid...Evelyn was terrified. She kept saying, 'What if it was ours?' So we never talked about it again."

"And you..." Jonas managed.

"I failed."

"But you did what you could."

"Yes. And I guess I learned to live with the idea that doing everything you can might not be enough." He stopped, gave Jonas a long, searching look. "Is that what you're dealing with? A sense of failure?"

"I lost some. I tried, but..."

"And that made you feel like a failure. Not your job, but *you*."

Jonas opened his mouth, but nothing came out. He ducked his head, closed his eyes, retreated from Doc's look.

Doc stood and put a hand on Jonas's shoulder. "Jonas, you are one of kindest, most compassionate people I have ever known. Unheard of in a person your age. You love people in the finest sense of the word. You want to make everything all right for everybody, even when you know you can't, and you try your damnedest even when it wrenches your guts out. For God's sake, don't ever lose that."

"But..."

Doc stopped him. "It's the curse of people like you and me to care, and to keep trying when we fail because we care. But you have to reconcile, Jonas, reconcile yourself to failure. Do all humanly possible, then let it go. If you can't do that, you either quit or go mad."

Jonas felt Doc's hand slip away, heard him cross the porch, the screen door open. Then he heard Doc say, "I'll tell you this, that boy — Francis — was not my biggest failure."

Jonas looked up. "What..."

But Doc was gone. Jonas rose, thinking to follow Doc, to ask, to demand. But instead, he sat back down, realizing he didn't want to hear any more about failure. Not right now.

* * * * *

Dinner with Gladys. She was in the kitchen, putting the finishing touches on curried chicken, when he got there. Pee Wee, the dog, was curled up in a small white ball at her feet.

"What can I do?" he asked.

"Did you pick up the habit of beer drinking when you were hanging around with those Marines?"

"Some," he said.

"Look in the fridge."

Amstel Light. Rodney's brand. Rodney had preferred the high test Amstel, but when he began to develop a sizable gut that cascaded over his belt line, he switched to the Light version. It didn't help. When Jonas and Fred Wesley were fourteen, they had pilfered two of them one evening, took them to the golf course and sat in a greenside bunker on Number Twelve. The taste was awful, but it was a matter of pride to get them down, feel the buzz at the edge of their brains that made them giggle. Turned out, Rodney counted beers. Jonas was grounded for two weeks.

He wandered now through the house with the beer, every room except his old one. He didn't care to be in there. Nothing of himself left in there. Again, as at Doc's and in town, things looked different, as if in his absence they had rearranged all the rooms. But probably not, he decided. Just a different way of looking at them, of pretty much everything now. And if you looked at things differently, didn't it mean that — for you — they truly were?

Back in the kitchen he asked, "Can that dog see?"

"Of course," she said.

"Why don't you get his hair cut?"

"He's happy with it just the way it is."

"How do you know?"

"He doesn't complain," Gladys said.

"Maybe he just sees what he needs to. Or wants to."

"It would," Gladys said, "be the sensible thing to do."

They ate on the patio, and that was different, too. Rodney had always insisted on dining at the dining room table. There was a table in an alcove that might have once been called a breakfast nook, but Rodney had always used it as a sort of home office, littered with lineup sheets and baseball books. It was off limits to Jonas. Now, on the patio, there was a wrought-iron table and four cushioned chairs.

"I don't remember this being here," Jonas said.

"Delivered yesterday," Gladys said. "It's nice to have some fresh air with your food, don't you think?"

Jonas thought about the months over there, MRE's on patrol. "Depends," he said.

He had been wary of coming, being grilled about himself; instead, she chattered about Copernicus people — her friends, his classmates. Cody Reighard, the first baseman he had smashed over the head with a lunchroom tray, was playing for Kansas City. Casper Knowlton, who had once had the local Chevy dealership, had lost his wife to an automobile accident in one of Casper's Chevrolets. He re-married, closed shop and moved to Waylonsville. Copernicus people now went to Waylonsville to buy their Chevys. Jonas only vaguely remembered Casper Knowlton. Rodney only drove Dodges.

There was dessert — blackberry cobbler, hot from the oven with a mound of vanilla ice cream. Gladys had always been a good cook. It was when they had finished the cobbler that Gladys asked, "Are you going to get the wheelchair ramp finished by Monday?"

"What's Monday?" he asked.

"When I'll need it."

"Mom, I don't have any idea how to build a wheelchair ramp."

"Then," she said, lips pursed, "figure it out."

He stared at her for a long moment before he thought, *My God, she's taking charge.*

It was Thursday evening. When he got back to Doc's, he called Fred Wesley. Yes, Fred Wesley said, he knew exactly how to build a wheelchair ramp, had in fact built one at Old Lady Reynolds' house just last month. On Friday, after Fred Wesley got off work with

Rayfield, they went to Glady's house and Jonas stood around while Fred Wesley did measurements and wrote stuff on the back of an envelope. Then they went to a lumber yard and filled the back of Fred Wesley's van with two-by-fours and sheets of plywood and galvanized nails. When they got back to Gladys's to unload there was a red Chevy van in the driveway.

"Whose?" Jonas asked.

"Mine," Gladys said. "Casper Knowlton delivered it himself."

"Mom, what is going on here?"

"What do you mean, Jonas?"

"All this..." his arm swept the yard, the house, the...

"Rodney can't walk, so he needs a wheelchair. A wheelchair can't get up the steps. The van has a wheelchair lift."

"And you've got a dog, and the van is a Chevy."

"Jonas," she said, hands on hips, "if you're just going to question everything I do, you might as well go back to Frank's house and let Fred Wesley build the ramp. Fred Wesley doesn't ask so many questions."

Jonas shrugged and gave up, and on Saturday, after Gladys had left in the red Chevy van to visit Rodney at the rehab center, he and Fred Wesley built the wheelchair ramp.

"It's a good thing you didn't have to use a hammer to play golf," Fred Wesley said. Jonas wasn't very good with a hammer, or any of the other tools it took to build the ramp. But he could fetch and tote, which he did with lumber and tools, and he could hold pieces of two-by-four and plywood on the sawhorses while Fred Wesley measured and cut. There was a sort of rhythm to it as the ramp began to take shape, with an undercurrent of the whine of the circular saw and the smell of fresh-cut wood and the sturdy sound of hammer against nail.

He studied Fred Wesley. Face fuller than in their youth, the lines smoothed, hairline beginning to recede. None of the scrunched-up forehead he remembered when Fred Wesley would bear down so intently on an idea that was hard to reach. Hint of a spare tire at his waist. Christy Jo's spaghetti, maybe. Jonas thought, *He has become a man — married, dependable, doing honorable work. A man at home with himself.*

By early afternoon, the ramp was almost done. The day was warm and they were down to tee-shirts. "Reckon your Mama has some Gatorade or something in there?"

Jonas smiled. "Better than that." And he fetched the last two bottles of Rodney's Amstel Light from the kitchen. They made short work of those as they cut the pieces of two-by-four for the railing and then Jonas made a pilgrimage to a convenience store for a six-pack. He was on the way back to the house when he realized that the clerk hadn't carded him. *Maybe*, he thought, *I look old and worn out. And not at home with myself.*

By the time the ramp was finished, he and Fred Wesley were pleasantly plastered. *Careful*, he told himself. *But just this once. With Fred Wesley…*

The ramp extended from the stoop at the side door next to the kitchen to the edge of the driveway. The railing was sturdy and the incline was manageable. Gladys had left behind the new wheel-chair she had brought home the day before, and Jonas and Fred Wesley took turns pushing each other in the wheelchair up the ramp to test it. Then they sat in the grass, their backs to a tree, and admired their work while they polished off the last of the six pack.

"How'd you learn to do all this stuff?" Jonas asked.

"Rayfield," Fred Wesley said. "I been working for him since we graduated. I was kinda fumble-fingered at first, but I just stayed at it."

"You have always pretty much stayed at it," Jonas said, "in general."

"I figure you can do pretty much anything you set your mind to if you just stay at it."

"I'll drink to that," Jonas said, and they clinked their beer bottles together. "You know, I couldn't stand the thought of beer for awhile. Bad memory. But now," he took another swig, "it's okay. Maybe it's the company."

"How about you?" Fred Wesley asked. "You got anything you have a mind to stay at?"

Jonas thought for awhile. "Nothing in particular."

"In the military, your Mama said you were some kind of a doctor."

"A long way from being a doctor," Jonas said. "More like a pills and band-aids guy."

They sat in silence for a while, and then Fred Wesley asked, "Were you handing out pills and band-aids when you got hurt?"

"I don't remember. I've been told that some people were shooting at us," he said.

"Who's us?"

"Me and some Marines."

"Why were they shooting at you?"

"I guess they were just pissed off that we were there."

"And you got shot."

"Once here," he fingered the place on his shoulder where you could feel the scar under his tee shirt, "and then here," he pointed to his hip. "And before the round went in my shoulder, it took off the two fingers." He stared at his left hand for a long moment and then a laugh bubbled up from somewhere. "It's a good thing it's not my jerk-off hand."

They both laughed at that because it took them back to an ancient time when they trudged along a fairway with Fred Wesley toting Jonas's golf bag and Jonas in a deep funk because he had just three-putted a green and lost his lead in the conference tournament.

"You know," Fred Wesley had said, "three-putting is like masturbation."

Jonas stopped in his tracks and stared at Fred Wesley, feeling a little pissed that Fred Wesley brought up a thing like masturbation when he was in such a funk for three-putting and losing the lead. "What?"

Fred Wesley grinned. "It's like masturbation. You're ashamed you did it, but you know you're gonna do it again."

"Where the hell did you hear that?"

"From Doc Ainsley. I was caddying for Doc and Daddy at the club last weekend, toting both their bags, and Daddy three-putted a green, and Doc said that thing about three-putting and jerking off, and I thought Daddy was gonna bust a gut laughing."

So Jonas and Fred Wesley had a good laugh there on the fairway and that took care of the tension and Jonas went on and birdied the last three holes and won the conference tournament. And as they walked off the eighteenth green together, Fred Wesley had said with another grin, "But you know, I ain't never been ashamed I did it." And Jonas, remembering what Doc had told him, agreed heartily with that.

Remembering it now, sitting under the tree in Glady's yard with a Saturday afternoon buzz on, they laughed together again. But then Jonas was hit with a rush of something that felt like sadness. Things far gone, lost, maybe irretrievable. Neither of them said anything for a long time. And then Fred Wesley got up and started collecting his tools and placing them carefully in his big gray tool box. Jonas started collecting scraps of two-by-four and plywood. There wasn't much of that because Fred Wesley had done a good job of figuring what they needed from the lumber yard. Jonas stood there with the scraps of wood in his arms and watched Fred Wesley and almost cried with envy. But he made himself not do that. When he finally spoke, it sounded lame, not nearly what he wished he could say but couldn't find the words for. "Fred Wesley Satterfield," he said, "you're a helluva dude."

Fred Wesley raised up from his tool box and gave Jonas a long look. "Are you gonna be all right, Jonas?"

And Jonas knew then that Fred Wesley — slow but not stupid Fred Wesley — knew things that might escape other people, even people who were supposed to be real smart. He knew a lot because he didn't try to know everything. And with somebody who knew that much, you couldn't be anything but honest. "I don't know, Fred Wesley," he confessed, "I really don't know."

"Well, whatever it takes, you do it, okay? And stay with it."

And Jonas said he would.

* * * * *

On Monday morning Doc said, "You need to go see Kayo Grissett." Kayo was the police chief, had been as long as Jonas could remember. He also coached the Little League baseball team, on which young Jonas had tried to play and failed miserably. But Kayo, he remembered, had never yelled at him like Rodney when he struck out or dropped an infield pop-up. Kayo showed up at all the high school sports events, even the golf tournaments. Representing the town, he'd say. It was understood that Mayor Fleetwood Satterfield, at three hundred pounds, didn't get around as well as Kayo.

"Why?" Jonas asked.

"I think," Doc said, "he wants to offer you employment."

Kayo was short and square, substantial belly, white hair in a crew cut. He wore a khaki shirt and pants with a Copernicus Police patch on one shoulder. No sign of rank except for the brass name tag on his shirt front that said CHIEF GRISSETT. And no pistol. He had a strong handshake and an easy smile that was somehow both firm and gentle, as if he'd rather talk you out of doing something illegal than arrest you.

"I'd like for you to think about coming to work for me," Kayo said when they were settled in his office.

"I couldn't shoot anybody," Jonas said.

Kayo laughed. "Shoot? I would hope not, Jonas. There hasn't been a shot fired by a sworn officer in Copernicus in decades, except at the range. But I don't want you as a sworn officer, I need you here in the office. Handle the radio and the phones and the walk-ins, keep things straight and orderly."

Jonas said, "I may not be staying."

"But you're here right now, and right now is when I need help. Tilda retired last week. Been here since Garfield was president, I think. In the short time since she's been gone, the place has become a mess."

Jonas shifted in his chair. "Why me?"

"Because you're the kind of fellow who can do the job. When you were growing up, I thought of you as put-together. That's how I remember describing you to your Mama one time. 'He's put-together,' I said to her. Looked the part, too. When you were playing golf, I never saw you without clothes so neat you looked like you just stepped out of the front window of Sikes Department Store."

"Mom made sure of that," Jonas said.

"I looked over your bag one time during a tournament. Every club spotless, in its own little plastic cylinder. And that's how you played, too. Closest thing to a spotless golf game I ever saw in a high school player."

"Did Doc put you up to this?" Jonas asked.

"Doc just told me you were back, and I thought about you and my job opening all by myself. I thought you'd be the kind of person who could fill it. Plus, you don't need to be just hanging around, doing nothing. Before you know it you'll be drunk and disorderly and I'll have to arrest you as a public nuisance. We've got enough public nuisances in town already."

"Can I think about it?"

"I can put you to work right this minute," Kayo said, "and right this minute is when I really need you."

"Do I have to wear a uniform?"

"No. Just dress neat and look like you know how to behave. Use your military bearing."

Jonas held up his left hand. "Is this a problem?"

Kayo took a quick look at the place where the fingers had been. "Might slow your typing a bit, but I imagine you'll figure it out."

"Well…"Jonas said, "…all right, then."

"Good. Are you gonna ask about pay and benefits?"

"Yes sir. What are the pay and benefits?"

"Adequate," Kayo said. "I'll work it out with the mayor and council. It won't be a lot to start, but if you work out, we'll see about some more down the line."

He stood and offered his hand again and Jonas took it. "Welcome to law enforcement," Kayo said.

They spent the afternoon going over the work — answering the phones, handling what little radio traffic there was with the two squad cars, one Kayo's, the other driven by the only other officer, a long-timer named Milo who had been with the force almost as long as Kayo. Both Kayo and Milo worked the day shift. When the day shift was over, the phones were routed to the county sheriff's department. If something happened that needed Kayo's attention, the sheriff's department would call him at home or reach him on the radio he kept in his kitchen. The phones, the radio, some filing of reports and such. Kayo would be close by if Jonas had questions or needed help.

"Copernicus is pretty quiet these days," Kayo said. "Back some years, it was what you might even call bustling. But with the plant gone..." His face flushed and he trailed off and Jonas silently finished it for him: *Gordon The Embezzler, the family shame.*

"Yes sir," Jonas said, trying to help, "it looks to me like Copernicus has shrunk. For sure."

"Used to be four thousand people in Copernicus," Kayo gave a shake of his head. "Now, barely three. But," he smiled, "those that are left deserve an efficient, well-oiled police department. And since you're here for awhile, you can help make sure it stays that way."

"Okay."

Kayo started to say something, hung fire, started over. "Jonas, I got to tell you, people are going to come by here. Not many know you're home, and only a handful know what happened to you. Frank Ainsley doesn't go around talking about his patients. But word's gonna get out. Folks are curious. I hope that's not gonna be a problem."

"I hope not," Jonas said after a moment. "I guess I've got to deal with it sooner or later. And this sounds like sooner."

"Yes it does. If it becomes a problem, if anything you're dealing with might affect what you do here, you tell me. Okay?"

"Yes sir."

"And one other thing. If you keep calling me 'sir,' I'm gonna start feeling like the old fart I am. Just call me Kayo. We're all adults here."

Jonas woke in the night, mind buzzing from whatever was back in its recesses — the whine of Fred Wesley's circular saw mingled with muffled explosions, flashes of fire, something at his throat. He fought the covers, gasping for breath, swung his feet over the side, sat there until his chest stopped heaving and his brain settled into a fragile hum. He thought about Kayo: *We're all adults here. Really? Kayo, obviously. Doc, of course. Fred Wesley, for sure. Kayo says I was a put-together kid. So, what happened that pieces fell off and now I feel like the absence of stuff, all hollowed out? It's truly fucking scary. But what's scarier than that? Maybe...finding out why.*

SEVEN

The doctors checked him over at the VA hospital. Everything healing, no unusual complications from his wounds. A prosthesis for his hand, the missing fingers? No, he'd stick with what he had. A different prescription to help him sleep, something for anxiety. He said he wasn't anxious, but they persisted. He thought he probably wouldn't take it. Unless things got out of hand.

Then there was the mental part. They could put him on a waiting list for a support group. He said he'd think about it. On the way back to Copernicus, he felt relieved. Kick that can down the road. Way down.

"Ain't no way I'm gonna be in a goddamn support group," he told Doc. "A bunch of guys sitting around dredging up shit? Getting into my shit? No."

Doc didn't argue. But several days later, Doc said, "The VA will approve your going to a private psychotherapist. They're working on the paperwork. Meantime, I want you to go see him. He's in Waylonsville. Next Tuesday."

"Aw hell, Doc…"

"Goddammit, Jonas, do it!"

He had never seen Doc quite that angry, never. So he did it.

✳ ✳ ✳ ✳ ✳

His name was Carl Lassiter. Early forties, wife and two kids, a PhD in clinical psychology from Chapel Hill.

"I've known Frank Ainsley for a long time," Carl said. "I grew up in Copernicus, and I thought I wanted to be a doctor. Frank let me hang around his place, do little things to help. End of the day, we'd sit down and talk about what I'd seen and done. I kept asking why people do the things they do — things that get them in trouble with their health and so forth. And finally one day Frank said, 'I think you'd make a good psychologist.' And so I did...well, good, you'll have to judge that for yourself. But Frank sent me in the right direction."

"What did he tell you about me?" Jonas asked.

"Only that you're someone he cares about a great deal and that you're toting some baggage around."

"Did he say I've got PTSD?"

"No, he didn't. The VA thinks you do, and maybe you do, but here at the start, I'm not into diagnosis. I may be a little unorthodox, something of a maverick, but I believe when you right off the bat get into diagnosis, then you're pretty quickly into 'Best Practices,' like if you follow those, everything will work. And if it doesn't, well it's not the fault of 'Best Practices.' I'm into what works. What works for you."

"Sounds like flying by the seat of your pants," Jonas said.

Carl smiled. "A trapeze act without a net."

"Then how do I know that you know what the fuck you're doing?"

Still, the smile. "You don't. But I'm not the one doing the work. You are."

Carl didn't have a couch. They sat in chairs, facing each other. Before Carl sat down, he picked up a note pad from his desk. He opened it now, pulled a ballpoint from his shirt pocket, clicked it back and forth a few times while he stared at the first, blank page. He finally looked up at Jonas. Cool gray eyes that seemed to latch on to you. "You've had combat trauma and you've watched a friend commit suicide."

"I don't remember the combat thing," Jonas said right away.

"Nothing?"

"Well, not exactly." Jonas told him about the gray, wispy figures out on the perimeter, beyond the wire. And then one of them becoming Willis, moving toward him, arms wide, getting swallowed up, falling...

Carl listened intently, leaning forward in his chair, making an occasional note on the pad that rested on his knee. When Jonas finished, Carl looked up. "Willis. Your sergeant."

"Yeah."

"The one who blew his brains out."

"Yeah."

"Do you think he was trying to get you to join him?"

"More like he wanted me to save him. And I couldn't. I couldn't move. And then he was gone."

"And the other figures?"

"Since the one I could make out was Willis, I guess maybe it was the platoon. Or what was left of it."

Carl did some more scribbling. "Do you feel safe, Jonas? Generally speaking?"

Jonas shrugged. "I'm not gonna off myself, if that's what you mean. I've got a good place to stay, Doc Ainsley, a job I just started. So…pretty much squared away."

"But there's all this other stuff, what you experienced, what you brought back with you. Those figures you talked about."

"Yeah. I don't sleep much. It's like…" he shrugged.

"Like what?"

Jonas hesitated. "Like, maybe if I give in, I'll get into some shit I don't want to get into."

"Give in to sleep."

"Yeah."

"So it's like playing defense."

"I guess that's it."

"It's incredible, what our minds can do," Carl said. "The same way with our bodies. We get a cut or scrape or," he raised his hand, "lose a couple of fingers, and the body starts trying to heal itself immediately. It might take a while to finish the job, but the defense kicks in right away. But it's like a football team. You can't keep the defense on the field too long. It gets worn down."

"Are you gonna help me play defense?" Jonas asked.

"Sounds like you're doing that pretty much on your own. I'd rather you have the ball and run some good offensive plays."

"This therapist at the hospital, she kept trying to get me to remember what happened when I got shot."

"How did you feel about that?"

"I got pissed," Jonas said. "I said I was doing okay not remembering."

"There are things you could try to help you remember," Carl

said, "hypnosis, sodium amytal — truth serum. Clinical trials with psychedelics that show some promise. One psychologist has had some success with farming. Dig some dirt, plant some stuff, grow it and eat it. Maybe leave some of the bad stuff in the compost pile."

Jonas said, "No thanks."

"Do you not want to remember?"

"Look Carl," he said, voice rising, "I got my ass shot off and some of the other guys got a lot worse than that. From what people keep trying to tell me, it was a true fucking shitstorm. Some didn't make it. I did. You think I want to go through that again?"

"Obviously, you don't."

"Are you gonna try to pull the same shit on me?"

Carl made a face. "It's one way to play offense. Reconnecting with trauma, or the memory of trauma, and doing it over and over until you eventually come to grips with it. It works for some people. But a lot drop out along the way because it's too intense. And some say it makes things worse."

"Well Carl, you won't have to worry about me dropping out, because I'm not going down that road to begin with. If you're gonna razz me about that like the woman at the hospital, we can just cut it all off right now."

He started to rise, but Carl said, "Then I won't." Jonas eased back in the chair.

"I told you," Carl said, "I'm into what works. You think that wouldn't work for you. So," he gave a jerk with his thumb over his shoulder, "that's out." He paused. "Unless you change your mind."

"Why would I do that?"

"Because what you don't remember will sneak up on you. From what you're telling me about your sergeant, those other figures, it's trying."

"I'll handle it. What else?"

"You tell me something that's bugging you, and we'll pick it apart and see if we can change the way you look at it." He paused, waiting. "So, what's bugging you?"

Jonas thought for a moment. "Everything looks different." He told Carl about his room at Doc's, the town, Glady's house. "People keep telling me it's the same as when I left, but it's like things got moved around while I was gone. They're in different places, or they've changed shapes, or something. Am I making any sense?'

Carl nodded. "They *are* different."

"What do you mean?"

"Because *you're* different. You're not the same guy who went off…what was it, three years ago…and had your life turned upside down. So now you're kinda looking at things upside down, or at least…"

"Cockeyed," Jonas said.

"New normal. It's your normal, like looking at people and things through the new set of eyes you got in Afghanistan."

"So do I just have to accept the new normal?"

"Recognize it for what it is. It's a different you. Doesn't mean it's better or worse than what your old normal was. It's just what is." Carl glanced at his watch. "Time. You've committed to fourteen weeks, once a week."

"Yeah."

"I can tell you're not at all sure about that."

"Depends on what you lay on me."

"No, it's what you lay on yourself. Jonas, you've got a couple of things going for you. From your training, you know something about fixing things that hurt. And, you're here. A lot of people who have the after-effects of trauma don't seek help because they see it as a stigma — a threat to their careers, a weakness, a blot on their manhood. You don't seem to have that problem. And I trust you when you say you have no thought of just ending things. If that changes, even in the slightest, hit the fire alarm. Don't try to deal with it by yourself. And if at any time you're tempted to use any kind of substance to help deal with it, you call me. Day or night." Carl reached for a card on his desk and handed it to Jonas. "Okay?"

Jonas took the card, glanced at it, nodded, put it in his shirt pocket.

"So we'll work from there. You don't have to do this by yourself," Carl said. "And if your sergeant Willis shows up again, tell him to kiss your ass."

Jonas stood. "Just one other question."

"Sure."

"Do you have other patients…like me."

"Yes."

"Have you lost any of them?"

Carl looked away for a moment. "Yes."

"So sometimes you fail."

Carl nodded. "Don't we all."

* * * * *

It started to rain as he was pulling out of the parking lot of
Carl's office, and as he headed down the two-lane it became a deluge
that made it hard for the wipers on the Honda to keep up. He was
maybe five miles from Copernicus when he saw the car on the side
of the road, an old Nissan with the trunk open, a woman pulling stuff
out. He slowed and eased onto the shoulder behind the car. When
the woman turned to look he saw that she was young and drenched,
shirt and jeans clinging to her body, long hair in messy strings. He
sat there for a moment, thinking that he had no umbrella or rain
gear. He got out.

She already had a jack out of the trunk and was struggling
with the spare tire. "Hi," he called out. The rain was in torrents,
drumming loudly on the car and pavement. He had to shout.

She turned on him, eyes flashing. "Mind your own fucking
business," she snapped.

He took a step back. "Whoa." The rain was plastering his
hair, dribbling down his chest and back. Thirty seconds, and he was
soaked. He tried again. "Can I help?"

"I don't need your fucking help." She pulled a tire tool out
of the trunk and waved it at him. "I've driven all the way from Texas
without anybody's fucking help."

"Look, it's okay. I'm not gonna mess with you. I'm…a police officer. Well, kind of."

"Go away and leave me alone. Go shoot some bandits or
something. Drink coffee." She turned back to the trunk, gave a
heave on the spare tire, and catapulted it out and onto the grass. He
peered around the side of the car and saw that the right front was
flat. He followed, keeping his distance, as she headed toward it with
the jack and tire tool. She knelt in the grass, shoved the jack under
the car, inserted the tire tool, and started pumping. The jack sank
into the sodden earth. She smacked her hand against the side of the

car and sat back on her butt. "Shit, shit, shit, double shit!"

He stayed a few steps back, but he said, "You need something under the jack."

"No shit, Sherlock. Maybe my head, huh? Or better yet, yours."

"I've got a piece of plywood in my car. That might do it."

She looked up at him, and it was then he realized that underneath her anger, she was pretty in a pinched sort of way. She stared at him, and then something gave way. "I can do it myself," she said hopefully, more a question than anything.

"I'm sure you can, but I'd really like to help. I'm harmless, but I know how to change a tire."

"Well hell," she gave the flat a karate kick, "give it a go."

She backed away from the car while he got the piece of plywood — just large enough to fit under the jack — and changed the tire. She stood back, silent, leaving him with the work. When he finished he took the flat to the trunk and laid it inside. The tire was nearly bald, and he saw that all of the others were too. Everything in the trunk was soaked, including a big duffel. He closed the trunk and looked over at her — back rigid, arms crossed across her chest, staring at the tire. The rain was easing up now. "I shoulda closed the trunk," he said. "Looks like your stuff got wet. Sorry."

She shrugged. "What the hell. I need a washateria anyway."

"There's one in Copernicus," he offered.

"Where's that?"

He pointed. "That way. You're almost there. You'll pass the washateria on the right just before you get to town."

She didn't say anything for awhile, then she opened the passenger door and reached inside for a wallet. "I'll pay you."

"Aw, hell no."

"You sure?"

"Yeah, I'm sure. Where you headed?"

"A gig."

"A what?" She pointed to the rear seat of the car and he peered through the window and saw a guitar case nestled on top of a pile of clothing and other stuff. "You a singer?"

"No, I play classical guitar with the New York Philharmonic," she said with a sneer.

"Okay. Well…"

He wanted to stay there a little while longer, talk to her, maybe get her to open up a little. *There's something about her…* She uncrossed her arms, gave a fierce shake of her head, hair flinging droplets of water, marched around the front of the car, opened the driver's side door, looked at him over the roof line. "Have a great life," she said, and got in, slamming the door behind her. The ignition ground in protest but then it caught and she pulled away, leaving him there feeling stupid and pissed and drenched. "And you're incredibly fucking welcome," he yelled after her.

* * * * *

Around four o'clock, Kayo sent him to the county sheriff's office to pick up some papers. The jail was next door, and as he passed it on the way to the office, she yelled from an upstairs window, "Hey! You with the plywood."

He looked up. Girl from this morning. Dry hair, but still stringy. Still the same pissed-off look. "What are you doing in there?"

"I got arrested, asshole. Whattaya think, I broke in? Get me out."

To hell with her. "I don't have my hacksaw with me."

"I'm sorry about this morning," she said, and he could tell she was trying to make it genuine, not entirely succeeding. "They made a mistake. Really. You said you're a cop."

"Well, not exactly. I work for the police chief."

"Don't quibble," she said. "Do something."

He stood in the corridor outside her cell, a jailer keeping an eye on them.

She clung to the bars. She looked pretty much diminished from this morning. "After you left, I drove into town and found the washateria. There was this guy in there and he asked for a ride. I said no. He pulled out a hundred. I said yes. Other side of town, some deputies pulled me over and went ballistic. Guns and everything. They hauled the guy out of the car, put him in cuffs, and drove off with him. Then they put cuffs on me and brought me here."

"Did they say what you're charged with?"

"No."

Downstairs, the sheriff told him what happened. They pulled her car because of the bald tires, and the guy she had in there with her was wanted for a triple murder in Tennessee. Armed and dangerous as hell. She'd be charged with transporting a fugitive across state lines.

"I know her," Jonas said. "She had a flat this morning up near Bentley Crossroads, I stopped to fix it. She was soaking wet, and I told her where the washateria was. She said the guy was in there, asked her for a lift. He wasn't with her when I stopped to help, so there's no way she could have transported him across the state line. She says she had no idea who he was."

The sheriff gave him a long look and scratched his crotch. Jonas had known him all his life. He was a school resource officer before he ran for sheriff, after the previous guy got caught in a prostitution sting. Rodney had campaigned for him. "We ran an NCIC on her," the sheriff said. "No record."

"I think it was just an innocent mistake, Sheriff."

"So…what, Jonas?"

"Let her go. I'll vouch for her."

"Well, she's gotta do something about those damn tires."

"You're a pain in the ass," he told her when they were outside at her car.

"I told you, I'm sorry. Look, you saved me a lot of grief. Twice in one day. Thanks. I really mean it." And this time she did seem genuine.

"What are you gonna do now?"

"What time is it?"

"Four-thirty."

"If I haul ass, I can make my gig tonight."

"Haul ass on bald tires."

"When I get paid, I'll get some new ones. Well, maybe some good used ones."

He fell silent for a moment, just looking at her. She really was sort of attractive in a scruffy kind of way. Early twenties maybe. Tall for a girl, about his height. He hadn't noticed that this morning, but then the rain had made her hunch over. She returned his look without blinking, and a little smile played at the edge of her mouth. "Can I go now, officer?"

"Aren't you gonna pay me?"

"For what?"

"I had to give the sheriff two hundred bucks."

"You're kidding."

"Yes."

She made a rude sound with her mouth, then climbed in the car. As she pulled away, she rolled down the window and said, "I'll remember you in my will."

* * * * *

Gladys called as he was getting ready to leave work. "I need your help," she said. "They're bringing Rodney. I can't handle him by myself."

His stomach lurched, his shoulders slumped. "I thought they brought him home yesterday."

"He had a bad day. They kept him over."

"Why did they wait so late in the day?"

"I don't know, Jonas," she said, exasperated. "All I know is that the ambulance will be here with him in fifteen minutes. And I need you. If you have something better to do…"

"No, Mom. I'll be there."

The ambulance was backing down the driveway when he parked at the curb. It stopped at the base of the ramp he and Fred Wesley had built, the doors swung open, and the two paramedics rolled Rodney out on a gurney and started up the ramp with him. Gladys was at the top of the ramp, holding the dog. Jonas stood back, watched, stunned at what was left of Rodney — shriveled and wasted under the sheet, face shrunken, hair gone gray. His eyes were closed, deep in the sockets. Jonas hadn't seen him in three years, and he wondered fleetingly what of Rodney's appearance was from the passage of time and what from the stroke. Mostly the stroke, he decided. Rodney had been six-three, more than two-hundred-fifty, with broad shoulders and a big head.

He followed the gurney through the side door, Gladys in the lead, showing them down the hall to a back bedroom, across from what had been Jonas's room. There was a hospital bed. He waited in the doorway while the paramedics lifted Rodney onto the bed and tucked him in. Then they were gone and Gladys stood there by the bed for a while — not touching Rodney, just petting the dog, a small white ball of fur. She seemed lost in thought. Then she looked up at Jonas, still in the doorway, and smiled. "I can take care of him."

"How?" he asked. "You said you couldn't do it by yourself."

"Not today. But I'll have help."

Not me, he started to say, but kept his mouth shut.

"The home health people will be here every day. And a therapist to continue his rehabilitation." She paused, pursed her lips, and then said, "He has a tube in his stomach."

"He can't swallow," Jonas said.

"They brought me some liquid thing. Three times a day in the tube. Maybe later, when he gets better, I'll puree some vegetables and put them through the tube."

Jonas shook his head.

She gave him a stern look. "Don't doubt me, Jonas. I've put up with far worse."

And, he thought, *you're damn right about that.*

He stayed for dinner. She had fixed a dish called Husband's Delight — lots of ravioli and meat sauce and cheese. It was one of Rodney's favorites, but despite that, Jonas liked it pretty well too. He tried to imagine her stuffing it down Rodney's tube.

Then there was dessert, pound cake with a scoop of ice cream. The cake was fresh from the oven and the ice cream was beginning to dribble down the sides. He had never been much into sweets, but he had always liked her pound cake. They ate in silence, and when she was finished she put her spoon down and said, "I wish…"

He knew exactly what she wished. "Mom," he said, "I can't do that. I just can't live here again. I've got to have my own space. And," he stopped short. What to tell her? "I'm dealing with some things from…" *What to call it?* "I'm seeing this psychologist in Waylonsville."

"And you can't find Waylonsville from here?"

"Look," he said, and he felt himself pleading but couldn't do anything about it. "I'm trying to sort through some things, what happened over there, and I can't deal with that and…" he gave a wave of his hand. *The house and all it contained — Rodney, bitterness, sense of betrayal,* "…this too. I've just got to take it one at a time."

Instead of protesting, as he expected, she reached across the table and took his hand. "Then do what's best for you. But don't stay away."

"I won't," he promised. "When you really need me, I'll come."

She checked on Rodney while he went to the patio. "Rodney's still asleep," she said when she joined him, sat next to him in the love seat, handing him a cup of coffee.

Then he felt a jolt of something, and he thought, *I have never heard her call him anything but Rodney.* Never *your dad,* always *Rodney.* "Why did you marry him?" he asked.

"Oh, my," she said with a sigh. He waited, and she finally took a sip from her own cup and set it aside. "Rodney was a catch."

"And that's all?"

She sat there in silence, looking out across the back yard toward the country club across the way, lights beginning to come on in the twilight. He knew the look, had seen it so many times when the air was filled with something difficult Rodney had said or done. Just stare off into space, looking beyond whatever was there into someplace where things weren't so much trouble. But then she took a deep breath and looked directly at him as if to say, *No more.* "Gordon," she said.

He waited. "Okay," he said, "Gordon, who stole you blind and went to prison."

"Not completely blind. Papa made sure of that. It's what he did to all those people at the plant. More than three hundred people lost jobs. Even though it's been years, some of them have never gotten over it. I see them in town and they look at me and it's partly sadness and partly hatred. We betrayed them."

"But that was Gordon, not you."

"It was the family. We helped build Copernicus. Always steady as a rock, doing things for the town — the country club, the senior center, things like that. When we failed, I felt ashamed. I still do."

He reached for her hand, but she pulled away and he realized she had gone rigid. "And then Rodney came back, and he was a sports hero and everybody was in awe of him, and he came courting. He rescued me."

He felt the anger rising. "He didn't rescue you, he was a shit to you."

"Don't," she said hotly, "ever use that word around me."

"He used it around you all the time."

"You're not him."

"No, thank God, I'm not. Why was he always like that?"

"He wasn't always."

"It's all I remember."

Her face softened. "At the first, he was…a lot better. And then…" She started to say something more, but stopped dead. He thought about Doc, on the edge of something he couldn't quite get out. What was it, with either of them? It wasn't a man behind the curtain, like in Oz, it was a *something*. Then he thought, *Who the hell am I, with my own something behind the curtain that nobody can drag out of me because, even though I know it's there, I'm not playing that game. So leave that, and this, alone.*

Now, whatever had made her seize up seemed to pass, and she reached for his hand with both of hers. She had always had soft hands, and in the days when he had felt so small and weak and helpless, such a failure in the hot glare of Rodney's disapproval, it was all she had had to give. It was something, but it wasn't nearly enough.

"I'm sorry," he said, and when he said it, he realized that what he meant was a great deal more than her shame and burden and the hollow place at the bottom of his own soul. It was, as he had thought standing there in Ray Willis's kitchen, a great aching sorrow for the whole fucking universal mess.

* * * * *

He found Doc in his study, engrossed in a book, which he put aside when he looked up and saw Jonas in the doorway. "Sit awhile?"

"Sure."

"How did it go today?"

He told Doc about Carl and the girl.

"Carl," Doc said. "You're okay with him?"

"He seems okay. Not in a rush to drag stuff out of me. He said he's known you for a long time. Grew up in Copernicus."

"Yes."

"And you steered him toward psychology."

Doc smiled. "He steered himself. All he needed was a nudge. Sometimes, that's all people need, a nudge." A moment, then Doc said, "Tell me about Rodney."

"He's..." he searched for a word, "...diminished."

"So I hear."

"Mom told me about marrying him, the plant and everything. But I kept thinking that there was something she was leaving out."

Doc's nose twitched. It was a moment before he said carefully, "Gladys has a lot on her plate. Always has."

"Well, she didn't rag on me about moving back in."

"You could be a lot of help to her if you wanted," Doc said. "Your training."

Jonas felt a stab of irritation. "They taught me how to plug holes in people, not take care of stroke patients."

"I guess that's true."

"Doc, was the thing with the plant, the closing, as bad as Mom seems to think?"

"Absolutely. It was, as much as anything, what made Copernicus tick. The people who worked there, the rest of the town that sold them things and doctored and lawyered and plumbed and carpentered and so forth. When it closed, you could feel the air go out of the town."

"Mom's still ashamed."

"I know."

"She's trying to…I don't know…make up for it somehow. Like it's a debt she can keep chipping away at, but won't ever be able to repay. Good deeds and stuff…"

"You think it's a guilt thing?"

Jonas shrugged. "I guess."

"Or maybe," Doc said, "there's more to it than that."

"Like?"

"Maybe, at heart, she's a caregiver. You know, there are people like that. Driven to give themselves to someone else, trying to make sure people are okay, have what they need. It can be a wretched way to live, because deep down you know you can't do a perfect job of it, but you're doomed to keep trying anyway."

"Well," Jonas said, "she's got her hands full now." He rose to go, feeling a rush of weariness, wanting nothing but a pill to drop him into the well of sleep where all of the fucking universal mess might stay somewhat at bay for a few hours.

But Doctor Frank Ainsley threw a monkey wrench into that when he said, "You're just like her."

EIGHT

Doc came by the police station early in the afternoon with a bag of tacos and they ate at Jonas's desk while he handled the radios and phones. Kayo Grissett came in, exchanged barbs with Doc, and then pulled up his right shirtsleeve and showed Doc a rash on his forearm. Doc looked, then showed Kayo's arm to Jonas. "What do you think?"

"Heat rash," Jonas said. "Ask Harvey at the CVS to recommend a cream or ointment and stop wearing those long-sleeved shirts. It's summer, Chief."

Kayo left for the CVS and Jonas and Doc finished their tacos. Doc cleaned up while Jonas took a call from a woman who thought her neighbor was spying on her and dispatched Milo to see about it. "Nice work," Doc said.

"Routine," Jonas said. "She calls about once a week. Sometimes it's the neighbor on one side, sometimes on the other. Milo goes over, spends a little time walking around her house, and tells her everything's all right."

"No, I mean the thing with Kayo's rash. You recognized what it was and gave him some good advice."

"I saw a lot of heat rash over there."

"And you took care of the old woman on the phone. I know who she is. A little crazy, but mostly alone and scared. You calmed her down, gave her some help. It's a gift you have."

"I'm not, as you said last night, just like my mother," Jonas said heatedly.

"Ever wonder why you became a corpsman when you went in the Navy?"

"I'm done with that! I'm done trying to fix things and people." He held up his left hand. "Last time I did, look what it got me. So drop it, Doc. If you bring it up again..."

"You'll leave?"

"Yeah."

Doc nodded. "I think you should. Get a place of your own. Depend on yourself."

"Okay," Jonas snapped. "I'll get my shit together this evening. There's a holding cell back yonder behind Kayo's office. I can sleep on the bunk."

"Calm down," Doc said evenly. "Wait till tomorrow. I've got some rental houses, and one of them just came vacant. It's a little bungalow, two bedrooms and a bath. Furniture, pots and pans, everything you need. It's yours if you want it."

Jonas sat there and thought about it and got himself calmed down. It might be nice, just his own space. "I've got money," he said, still on edge.

"Of course," Doc said. "It's called 'rental.' Three hundred a month."

"That's not much."

"It's what it's worth. Needs some work."

"I'll take it." He ducked his head. "I didn't mean to sound like an asshole."

"Apology accepted. I'm glad you're sticking around. In Copernicus. You had talked about not staying."

"I still might not."

"But for a while. Until you get your wheels back under you."

"And there's Mom," Jonas said.

Doc didn't say a thing. He just smiled.

* * * * *

It was a neat little house on a quiet street a couple of blocks from the high school. Older homes and mostly older people who had lived in Copernicus a long time and drove (when they went out at all) lumbering boats of cars, Buicks and Chevys. Several dropped by with some sort of gift from their kitchens — casserole, apple pie, fresh bread — to welcome him to the neighborhood, ask how he was doing, inquire about Rodney. He had known most of them, or at least about them, all of his life, and they had known him. He answered their questions politely. *Yes ma'am, I was over there for awhile. Nothing*

Robert Inman   95

serious. Glad to be home. Rodney? Doing okay, Mom's taking care of him.

The street had a scattering of younger couples with small kids, tricycles on the sidewalk, play sets in the back yard. There would be more of the young. The day after he moved in, there was an ambulance in front of Woodrow Parker's home, and then Woodrow on a stretcher, covered by a sheet. Polly, his widow, wouldn't be around much longer.

He got right away into the habit of going for late walks, feeling the day's heat still radiating from concrete and asphalt, moving quietly among the shadows cast by street lamps through the tall old trees. Most of the old folks had their lights out by then, but there was the warm glow from the windows of the younger and the dancing fluorescence of the *Late Show*. Even with the tricycles and gym sets, it felt like time moved slowly here, especially as the weather warmed. He had been back for two months. For now, it was okay to stay.

The house had a scraggly front yard, red dirt showing through the Bermuda, but he found a lawnmower in the shed out back and trimmed it. The shrubbery in the front of the house needed pruning, and he thought he might get around to that.

The back yard was small but fairly neat, private, hemmed in by hollies and arbor vitae. Two old Adirondack chairs, a small rickety table, a fountain that didn't work. A couple of times, Doc dropped by, but he mostly had the place to himself and in the evenings he sat out back letting the day fade, munching on whatever take-out he had picked up on the way from work. There was a TV inside, but he wasn't much interested. He had no computer, nor any interest in one. Only Doc, Kayo, Gladys, Fred Wesley and Lieutenant had his cell phone number, and besides, he was often without the phone. It was quiet here and he could ease down into *Don't-think*, his *area*, all squared away.

He went to Gladys's after work. She, too, seemed squared away. The home health people came daily — bathed Rodney, got him up and in the wheelchair. When Jonas got there in the late afternoon, he would be in the den with the TV on to some sports channel or another. He was mute — the stroke had done that — but his eyes followed Jonas, who stayed long enough to get him settled for the evening, helping Gladys move him from the wheelchair to the bed. What there was left of him was dead weight, but much less of it than had been. The physical Rodney was a shell of the tyrant Jonas remembered, and he found himself letting go of some of the old bitterness. If Rodney could speak, what would he say? Would there be the same old poison? No way of knowing. A physical therapist came three days a week, helping Rodney move his limbs. The doctors had told Gladys that he might recover some of his mobility within a year. For now, there wasn't much more than just the eyes, and they didn't reveal much of what was left in the physical shell.

Sometimes, he stayed for supper. Gladys asked questions. He was wary at first, keeping his distance, but he began to open up a bit — his job, his wounds, Carl the psychologist Yes, he said, he probably had PTSD. She had been reading about it in a book she got from the library. She didn't push, didn't pry, let him reveal what he was willing on his own. So they talked. But there was a lot he didn't remember. And hoped he never did.

Lieutenant called the police station just before five. "Come out here," he said. "I want you to see something."

"What?"

"I'll show you when you get here. It's a matter of national security."

"Bullshit."

"Just come. Unless they've got you guarding a bunch of serial killers."

"In Copernicus?"

There was a scattering of people at the mats. Lieutenant was giving a lesson to a woman who was so fat she couldn't see the ball when she took her stance. Jonas sat in the gazebo and watched. The woman swung as mightily as a fat woman can. The tip of the club nicked the ball and it rolled about five yards to her right. She peered way downrange as if expecting to win a long drive competition. Lieutenant looked back at Jonas and rolled his eyes, then said to the woman, "You're gettin' there. Hit the rest of this basket of balls and work on what we've been talking about."

He started toward the gazebo, pointing to the far end of the range. "Down there," he said. It was the lanky kid from the other day, flailing away at ball after ball, sending the shots in all directions except straight. There was a stubborn anger to it, something almost at the level of rage.

"I'm afraid he's gonna hurt himself," Lieutenant said. "See if you can talk some sense into him." Lieutenant veered away and headed toward the pro shop.

Jonas watched for a couple of minutes until the kid ran out of balls, then turned with a jerk, slammed the club into his bag, picked up the bag, and started toward the parking lot.

As the kid passed the gazebo, Jonas thought, *Let the little twerp go. I'm through with all that stuff.* But before he could catch himself, he said, "It's not as bad as it feels."

The kid stopped in his tracks. "What…"

"You're not all that far off. With some work, you could be okay."

The kid was about five-ten, beanpole skinny, long arms, long fingers, pimpled, slump-shouldered like kids are when they've outgrown themselves. He was wearing a Polo shirt frayed at the collar, faded plaid shorts. "Who are you?" he asked.

"The best golfer who ever came out of Copernicus High School."

"Yeah?"

"Yeah."

"So?"

"How long you been swinging a golf club?"

The kid took a couple of steps back, and Jonas thought for a moment he might cut and run. But then he said, "Few months."

"Not getting any better?"

"What does it look like."

"Train wreck," Jonas said.

"Fuck you." The kid gave a fierce shake of his head and marched off.

"I could help," Jonas called after him, and then said to himself, *Don't do this, Jonas. Mind your business. You can't fix things.* But…"I could have you swinging like a pro in a month." *Goddamn, Jonas. You just can't fucking help yourself.* But the kid kept going, pounding hard toward the parking lot, back and shoulders rigid, the golf bag banging against his side. Jonas felt a rush of relief. *Dodged that one.* He sat back down in the gazebo and felt the hard knot in his gut slowly relax. He thought about Ray Willis. *A fucking do-gooder*, Ray had called him. Is that what it was, whatever had happened over there? Or something else? If he had really done what they said he had done…

Then the voice at his back. "Okay."

Jonas turned to see the kid standing there, glaring down at him. Before Jonas could speak, the kid walked over to a mat, set his bag down, pulled out a club, and stood there with his back to Jonas, waiting. Jonas felt his gut tightening again — felt like now, he might be the one to cut and run. Instead, he took a deep breath, stood, and went to the mat. "Put the club away," he said.

"Don't you wanna see…"

"I saw. Put the club back in your bag."

The kid held onto the club. "Look, if you ain't gonna help me swing a golf club, just say so. What are you, some kinda pervert, picking up kids?"

"How old are you?" Jonas asked.

"Fuck you," the kid said. Then, "Fourteen."

"Trashy mouth, piss-poor attitude, and a swing that flies off in all directions at once. That's a helluva collection of shit for somebody who's only fourteen."

"Fuck you."

Jonas took a step toward him. "You know what, I think I'll just whip your ass and be done with it."

The kid backed away, raising the club. "I'm as big as you are, shitass, and I've got a golf club."

Jonas laughed. "So what. I'm a U.S. Marine and an expert in karate."

The kid just stared. "No you ain't."

"Go ask Lieutenant."

The kid marched off to the pro shop. He was back in a couple of minutes with a strange look on his face. "Lieutenant said you know five ways to kill a person with just your fingers."

"Four, actually." He held up his left hand. "I'm missing a couple of fingers."

The kid stared. "How'd you get that?"

"Bar fight. Now, do you want to have a go at me, or are you gonna let me help you with that miserable attempt at a golf swing?"

"F…" the kid started, but checked himself. He jammed the golf club back in his bag.

Jonas stuck out his hand. "Jonas."

"Ben," he said. His grip was soft, wary. He avoided Jonas's eyes.

"Okay, Ben. What you've got, we can work with. For now, we'll work on just one thing. If that helps, fine. If not, you can fire me."

"I can't pay," Ben said.

"Is that why you won't let Lieutenant help you?"

"Maybe."

"Well, we'll figure something out."

They worked for a half hour, Jonas showing him how to set up properly, shoulders and hips square, spine straight, weight balanced, grip firm but light. Set up, get ready to swing, then step away, shake everything loose, do it again. When Jonas was done, he said, "That's it."

Ben gave him an odd look. "Don't you want me to hit a ball?"

"No, I definitely do *not* want you to hit a ball. Do you feel what it's like when you set up right?"

"I guess."

"Don't guess. Show me."

He did. Not perfect, but passable.

"That'll do. Go home and practice. Over and over. Without the club, and then add the club but don't swing. Just set up. Train your muscles and your brain so it becomes automatic. When you've got that, we can work on something else."

"Tomorrow?"

It took him by surprise. *God, the kid looks hungry. There's a lot of anger, but underneath… What am I getting myself into?*

"I can be here at four," Ben said.

"I don't get off work until five. And then sometimes I help my Mom for awhile."

"Six?"

"Well…"

"If you don't want…"

"No. Six. Tomorrow."

Villages

Ben hoisted his bag, ducked his head. "Thanks." He seemed to have a hard time getting it out. Maybe having somebody help — with anything — didn't come easy. Jonas remembered what Lieutenant had said about the kid's situation, his mom.

Ben started away and Jonas called after him, "How'd you get out here?"

Ben kept walking. "Bike."

"You mean you rode a bicycle out here from town with your golf bag?"

"What about it?"

"You do that every time?"

"Yeah." And then, again to Jonas's surprise, there was a little hint of a smile. "My Mercedes is in the shop."

"Well, my Honda's over yonder."

It was a down-at-the-heels, rust-streaked mobile home, hunched like war wreckage among a riot of weeds and junk. In the yard, between where the rutted gravel driveway ended and the trailer began, a butt-sprung sofa, couple of tires, a see-saw with its back broken, an ancient refrigerator with the door off. Jonas pulled to a stop and sat there for a moment looking things over, Ben silent in the passenger seat, scrunched up against the door, looking away from him. He climbed out and opened the trunk.

"I'll get the clubs," Jonas said.

"No," Ben snapped. "I got 'em."

He could tell the kid wanted to get away from him, want-ed him to go away, was sorry he accepted the offer of a ride, sorry Jonas was seeing the shit-pile where he lived. He wheeled the bike to the trailer, propped it against the side, and came back for the clubs. Jonas was looking them over — an ancient set, pitted heads, grooves worn, grips frayed. A set of initials stamped into the metal heads of the two wedges: **B.L.** "Where'd you get the clubs?" he asked.

Ben indicated the trailer with an impatient jerk of his head. "In there."

"Somebody give 'em to you?"

"No, I just found 'em." He lifted the bag out of the trunk.

"Tomorrow at six."

"Yeah. Look, if you don't want to mess with me..."

"Same here."

Ben shrugged. "I guess it's okay."

Ben turned to go, and just then the door of the trailer swung open and a man stood there — scrawny, pot-bellied, unshaven, unruly hair, wearing boxer shorts and a sagging t-shirt, holding a beer bottle. Ben froze and Jonas glanced at him, saw fear and loathing etched in the kid's face.

"Your dad?" Jonas asked.

"Hell no. Oscar."

"Friend of your Mom?"

"Yeah."

"Hiya kid," Oscar called out, waving the beer bottle. "Help you with anything?"

"No," Ben said. His voice cracked. "I got it."

Jonas took a step toward Ben. "Is your Mom here?"

"I don't know. She might be at work."

"Are you okay...with this?"

Ben whirled on him, flaring. "I'm fine. Go away."

"Want me to pick you up tomorrow?"

"No! Fuck off!"

Jonas was stunned by the vehemence of it, but he saw that it had nothing to do with him, or with golf, but with whatever wretched thing the kid was dealing with in his private shit-hole. He wanted to grab Ben, push him back in the car, get the hell out of here. But he couldn't, he had no right, and that made something come loose inside him. Ben shouldered the bag and headed for the trailer. Oscar stepped back, let him in, and closed the door. Jonas stood rooted in place, feeling an ancient poison churning his belly.

He backed away, banged hard against the side of the Honda, stumbled to the driver's side, reached for the door handle, snatched it open, tumbled in.

He was shaking hard, gasping for breath, head spinning, then there was the fire and explosions and he was someplace that people wanted to kill him.

He fell out of the car, sprawled in the weeds on all fours, retching his guts out.

And then it passed, leaving him so weak and terrified he could only roll onto his side and lay there for awhile. He managed finally to crawl back in the car, turn the key, put it into reverse. He took one last glance at the trailer. A curtain pulled back, then closed quickly. He drove away.

Lieutenant was unpacking a box of new Titleists, stacking them on a shelf behind the cash register, humming "Sweet Georgia Brown." He glanced up as Jonas walked in, kept working.

"What are you trying to do to me?" Jonas demanded.

"Do?"

"You're trying to reel me in, aren't you."

"Take a load off, Jonas. I'm busy."

Jonas hesitated, then pulled up a stool. Lieutenant took his time, finished emptying the Titleist box, then turned, gave Jonas a long, searching look. "Look at yourself, Jonas. You've let yourself go to seed. Your hair's too long, you got that mangy excuse for a beard, your clothes look like you borrowed 'em from the Salvation Army, you're so skinny you don't cast a shadow. You get up every morning and go work for Kayo, then you go home and hide. Whack off, feel sorry for yourself, I don't know what you do, but nobody sees you after five o'clock in the afternoon. People ask about you, know you're home, but they don't see you."

Jonas started to lash out at him, but Lieutenant held up a hand. "Look," he said his voice quieter now, "I know what it's like to come back with your head either full of shit or just plain empty. You're going to a shrink, and I hope he's helping. I wish somebody — like maybe the VA — had helped me, but that was mostly my fault. After 'Nam, nobody was talking much about how combat fucks you up. We just mostly dealt with it on our own, and I did it by buying up some land and throwing myself into it. This place saved my life, Jonas. There were times when I was so screwed up I thought a bullet in the brain was the answer. But then I'd come out here and get on the tractor and push dirt, sometimes in the middle of the night. Then when I had it carved out the way I wanted, I looked it over and said, 'This is worth living for.'"

"And how the hell am I supposed to do that?"

"Climb out of your foxhole and go looking. *Do* something outside yourself. Probably doesn't matter what it is. Form a tiddly-winks club, join Rotary and do good stuff. Help a kid. Or…play golf."

Jonas raised his left hand.

"Yes, you can," Lieutenant insisted. "Hell, blind people play golf. People with no legs or arms play golf. Come out here tomorrow with your clubs and I'll prove that you can."

"I don't think so."

"Sleep on it. Now, help me unpack the rest of this stuff. Make your sorry ass useful."

They worked together for a bit and Jonas felt himself easing away from the thing that had spooked him back there at the trailer. Getting squared away.

"How did it go with the kid?" Lieutenant asked after awhile.

"Okay. Worked on setup."

"And?"

"You ever been out there…where he lives?" The thought of the trailer made him queasy. He swallowed hard, trying to keep the bile down.

"No," Lieutenant said, "but I've heard about it."

"There's this guy. Oscar."

"Latest of many. I told you about his mother."

"It looked scary. I wanted to grab the kid and run."

"Makes you want to hit something, don't it."

"Yeah," he said.

Lieutenant turned to him, put a strong hand on his shoulder. "Try doing it with a golf ball. Do with it what you used to do."

"What?"

"Knock the piss out of it." Then Lieutenant hugged him. Lieutenant had never hugged him before. But he realized how much he needed it just now, and figured that Lieutenant realized it, too.

* * * * *

"Doc…Doctor Ainsley…says I'm a caregiver," Jonas said to Carl.

"Are you?"

"He said that's why I became a corpsman. He said I'm doomed to try to help people, even when it gets me in trouble."

Carl nodded, made a note on his pad. "Has it gotten you into trouble lately?"

Jonas told him about Ben.

"You say you really didn't want to help him, but you did anyway?"

"I guess. I opened my big mouth."

"Do you regret it?

Jonas shrugged. "The kid's got trouble. I don't think anybody else is doing much for him."

"So you are."

"Just the golf, that's all. I can't get into the mess he has at home."

Carl smiled. "Do you have a soft spot in your heart for kids?"

"Maybe."

"Do they remind you of you?"

Jonas thought about that for awhile. Instead of answering, he told Carl about the village.

The company FOB was a half-mile from the village. It had been pretty much busted up in a series of firefights. Quiet for now, but they were cautious — on edge, waiting for something bad to happen. The first time Jonas patrolled with a squad from the platoon it seemed deserted. There had been some mortar fire earlier, back and forth, and there were signs of fresh damage. Then he began to get the feeling of being watched, and when he looked out of the corners of his eyes he could spot a quick flash of faces at the windows of the less-damaged homes. Small faces with large, furtive eyes.

They turned a corner and there was the kid, out in the street. The squad stopped and went into defensive crouch. Sometimes a lone kid could mean an IED nearby, especially a kid like this one with no legs. But this kid was crying, just sitting there, face shiny with tears. He looked at the Americans, and that was when they saw the raw, angry scrape on the side of his face. The legs had been gone for a while, pants tied just below the stumps, but the scrape was new.

Jonas moved to the front of the patrol, up where Willis was all business, watching the kid, the street, the rooftops. Willis knew what to look for — freshly disturbed earth, an animal carcass, an old car fender.

"Sarge," he said, "let me go take a look at him."

"And get your ass blown off? I don't think so."

"I don't see anything suspicious. It might've been one of our mortar rounds."

"Somebody'll come for him."

"But they probably don't have anything to treat the wound. It'll get infected."

"Boulware, are you arguing with me?"

"Yes, sergeant."

Willis sat back on his haunches, passed a hand over his face. He looked like crap — no sleep, lots of stress, trying to keep them all safe. He let out a long breath. "Okay. I'm going with you."

So they went at a low crouch, the rest of the squad moving into position behind them, everybody's assholes puckered up tight. About ten yards or so from the kid, Willis grabbed his sleeve and they stopped and looked things over. The kid's eyes were locked on them, huge and terrified. "He's okay, sarge. Just hurt and scared." And then Jonas realized how scared *he* was — mouth dry as dust, heart galloping. It was beastly hot, and Jonas could feel rivers of sweat coursing down his face, his neck and shoulders. Finally Willis nodded and they went to the kid, who recoiled, as much as you could without legs, shrinking into himself. He was crying hard, but there was no sound to it. Jonas put a hand on the top of the kid's head, managed a smile, stayed like that for awhile until the kid calmed down a little. "Hey," he said, forcing his voice to stay calm, "it's okay." He wished he knew something in Arabic. Then he remembered the pack of Lifesaver mints in his pocket, dug it out, offered the kid one. He hesitated, but Jonas nodded and kept the smile going, and finally the kid reached out, took it, slipped it in his mouth. Willis gave Jonas an impatient look, but he ignored it.

Jonas slipped off his assault pack, pulled out what he needed, and tended the kid's scrape — cleaned it, applied antibiotic ointment and a bandage. There had to be some sting to it, but the kid was stoical, his eyes fixed on Jonas. When he was finished, he closed up the pack, put his hand on the kid's head again and gave him another smile and the rest of the Lifesavers. He sat back on his haunches. "Where do you live?" he asked, arm sweeping the surrounding area. The kid seemed to understand and pointed to the ruins of a building thirty yards or so down the street. There was a gaping hole where the door had been, a lot of debris in the street in front.

Jonas picked the kid up. He weighed almost nothing. Willis was on his feet in an instant. "What the fuck do you think you're doing?"

"Taking him home." And he started off toward the building.

"Goddammit!" Willis motioned the rest of the squad forward and half of them formed a defensive perimeter around the front of the house while Willis and the other half burst inside. Jonas held the kid and stared at the hole where the door had been and after a moment realized that he could see sunlight inside the hovel. The roof was gone. And then Willis walked out, looking wretched. He knelt and pulled off his helmet. The other squad members followed him out and one of them bent at the waist and vomited against the ruins. The others were ashen, wasted. "Direct hit," Willis said quietly.

Jonas looked at the kid cradled in his arms. *What the fuck are we doing here, eating each other alive?*

They searched the village and found some adults who took the kid with them. And they saw how many other kids were still there, families hanging on because they had no choice.

Jonas began to make regular trips to the village, accompanied by a couple of guys from the platoon, to do what he could. Did it, that is, until Lieutenant Hammer took over the platoon and made him stop. *Goddamn Lieutenant Hammer.*

Carl said quietly, "That was a hard story to tell."

"Not," Jonas said, "as hard as it was to live it."

"Lieutenant Hammer. He was…"

"A sonofabitch," Jonas said.

"What about him made you feel that way?" Carl asked.

"Because he was. Stuff he did, the village, the platoon, and…" But that was as far as he could go. Yes, there was something else about Hammer, but he couldn't go there. A place that was shut off behind a curtain of fire and explosions and death. "I don't remember," he said.

And then it just came out, words tumbling over each other in a torrent — the thing at the trailer, the flashback, the terror of it. It took just a minute, but when it had passed, he realized he was ramrod-backed on the edge of his chair, fists clenched, every inch of his insides tied in knots. He slowly opened his hands, slumped back, exhausted with it.

It was a couple of minutes before Carl said anything. "Is that the first time it's happened?"

'No."

"You know what's going on, Jonas."

He nodded.

"You're trying to keep your finger in the dike."

Another nod.

"But when something reminds you — the kid and the golf, the kid in the village, it's a trigger. The pressure builds, the hole in the dike gets wider, and all hell breaks loose."

Jonas stared at his hands, then squeezed his eyes shut. After a moment, "What can I do?"

"Watch for the triggers — the situations that remind you of all this you're trying to keep at bay. Get help. From the nearest person you trust. And let me know. Immediately"

"Okay." He stood, holding onto the arm of the chair. A couple of deep breaths. *Get me the hell out of here.*

"I'll see you in a week," Carl said, laying his pad aside. "Meanwhile, try to be easy on yourself. Ask yourself, 'Can I help the people I'm desperately destined to help without putting myself in harm's way? What's the price of opening up?'"

* * * * *

It was just after ten when Kayo called. "We've got a hostage situation," he said.

"You want me to go to the station?"

"No," Kayo said, "I need you here."

"Where?"

"Fred Wesley's house."

The small white frame house was lit up like a Cape Canaveral launch pad by a bank of spotlights. Cop cars everywhere — police, sheriff's department, state troopers, an ambulance and a fire truck. A lot of cop types, crouching behind cars. A lot of weapons. A gaggle of people on the sidewalk on the other side of the street. There was a loud staticky noise that Jonas realized, as he got closer, was a bullhorn. And then he saw that Mayor Fleetwood Satterfield had the bullhorn, but his mouth was too close to it, and he was talking too loudly, and you couldn't understand a thing he said. Like the *wah-wah-wah* in the Peanuts comic strip. Fleetwood finished and passed the bullhorn to Kayo as Jonas walked up.

"See if you can talk some sense into him," Kayo said. "Maybe he'll listen to you."

Jonas jammed his hands in his pockets. "What's going on?"

"Some kind of argument and Christy Jo's mother got into it, and now Fred Wesley's holding them hostage. He's armed and dangerous."

"Fred Wesley?"

"He came to the door once and he had a gun in his hand. That's when I called in reinforcements."

Jonas looked around. Some of the sheriff's guys in riot gear. He doubted the Copernicus Police Department even had riot gear. Kayo looked like he was on the verge of hyperventilation. His eyes were a little bloodshot and there was high color in his face.

Mayor Fleetwood Satterfield looked stoic. "I was afraid it would come to this," Fleetwood said.

Jonas started across the lawn toward the house.

And then it wasn't a lawn, it was a street in a village, long and narrow with a fucked up car on one side and rubble on the other. Behind him, noise — screams, explosions, concussions, people yelling — that shoved him in the back, propelling him forward. Reaching for his assault pack. Not there. He was sprinting now. Stumbled. Picked himself up. Ahead, the mortar-blasted house with the kid inside. And then...

Fred Wesley. *What?!* "Jonas, what are you doing here?"

"I don't know." And he didn't.

Fred Wesley grabbed his arm, pulled him inside the house,

closed the door. "Jonas, you look white as a sheet. Come here and sit down." Fred Wesley led him to a sofa, pushed him down, stood over him. "Are you okay?"

Jonas shook his head. "Give me a minute."

Fred Wesley sat down in a recliner. "Take your time."

It took a couple of minutes, but he came to himself — shaken, the air sucked out of him. He looked around. Fred Wesley in the recliner, the TV set on, a Braves game. From somewhere in the back of the house, a banging sound.

"Fred Wesley…"

"Yeah?"

"What's going on?"

"Braves are behind three-to-two. Last of the sixth."

"Kayo said you're armed and dangerous."

"I don't like guns," Fred Wesley said matter-of-factly.

"But do you have one?"

"Of course not, Jonas." Fred Wesley picked up the TV remote. Black plastic. "You want me to change the channel?"

"No," Jonas said weakly. "Braves game is just fine, Fred Wesley."

They watched the Braves game for a few minutes and then Jonas said, "What's that banging back yonder?"

Fred Wesley smiled. "I got Christy Jo and her mama locked in the bathroom."

"That's interesting."

"Me and Christy Jo had an argument. But we was doing all right until Maylene come over here and stuck her snout in it."

"Maylene?"

"Christy Jo's mama."

"What were you arguing about?"

Fred Wesley hit the mute button on the remote. "Spaghetti. I come in from work and Christy Jo was fixing spaghetti, third time this week and it's just Wednesday, and I pulled a TV dinner out of the refrigerator and she got all huffy about that and said, 'Are you too high and mighty to eat my spaghetti?' And I said, 'I love your spaghetti, honey — I usually call her honey when we're having an argument — but how about a little variety.' Mama told me when we got married, it's important that you choose the right words when you're talking to the person you marry, so I used the word variety."

The sound of Fred Wesley's voice, stringing out the story, calmed Jonas. On familiar ground now. Whatever it was outside, still outside. The lights, making a halo of the drawn shades, the bullhorn. "Sounds like it fit the situation, Fred Wesley."

"So I come in here and ate my TV dinner and Christy Jo called Maylene. And she come over and stuck her snout in it."

"So you locked 'em in the bathroom?"

"Stuck a chair under the knob."

"Does Maylene have her cell phone with her?"

"Yep."

"You know she called 911."

"Yep."

"And there's a big ruckus outside."

"Yep. And I don't rightly know what to do about that, Jonas. It's done got kinda out of hand, I guess. My daddy and all of 'em out there with their panties in a wad."

"That's about right, Fred Wesley."

Jonas thought about it for a couple of minutes while the Braves scored a run and tied the game. "Would it be all right if I tried to get things straightened out?"

"I'd be obliged, Jonas. I really would be obliged."

Jonas got up and went in the back to the bathroom. He could hear Christy Jo and Maylene in there talking. He knocked. "Christy Jo?"

Silence. "Are you the police?"

"Jonas."

"Oh. Get us out of here."

"Did you call 911 Christy Jo?"

"Mama did."

"Maylene, did you tell 'em that Fred Wesley is armed and dangerous?"

More silence. Then, "I might have."

"Do you realize, Maylene, that it might amount to filing a false police report? And that you could be in big trouble for that?"

"Huh. What do you know?"

"Well, I work for the police department."

"Oh."

"I'm gonna open the door now, and I'm going out to the street and tell Kayo that it was all a mistake. Are you all right with that?"

"All right," Maylene said after a moment.

"Christy Jo?"

"Well, Fred Wesley has got to apologize about the spaghetti."

"He just did. Told me he was really sorry about that."

"Okay."

Jonas removed the chair from under the doorknob and went out to the street where Kayo was almost jumping up and down with excitement. Probably, Jonas thought, the closest thing to excitement in Copernicus in a long time. Fleetwood weighed too much to jump up and down. "He's not armed and dangerous," Jonas said.

"But he had a gun in his hand when he came to the door," Fleetwood said.

"The TV remote."

When Jonas went back inside with Kayo and Fleetwood, Christy Jo and Fred Wesley were curled up together in the recliner and Maylene was back in the kitchen. Christy Jo and Maylene said it was all a big misunderstanding and Kayo went back to the street to tell the sheriff's boys and the troopers to go home. And then Maylene said there was plenty enough spaghetti, and did Jonas want to stay for dinner? So, even as late as it was, Jonas did.

The next morning, when Jonas went to work at the police station, Kayo was bleary-eyed and out of sorts. "That was a damn fool thing you did, Jonas," he said. "What were you thinking?"

"I don't guess I was," Jonas admitted. He didn't tell Kayo about the village and the explosions.

Kayo shook his head and then went back in his office and rattled around awhile and then came back to Jonas's desk. He pulled up a chair and sat down. There wasn't any radio traffic this morning and the phone hadn't rung a single time since Jonas got there. "Jonas," Kayo said, "I called you because you and Fred Wesley have been friends for a long time. And I always admired you for that. Not everybody was nice to Fred Wesley when y'all were in school together, but you always stuck with him."

Villages

"My best friend," Jonas said agreeably.

"That's why I called you."

"Like you said."

"I didn't expect you to go off half-cocked like that. You coulda got shot."

"By a TV remote?"

"No, by some trigger-happy law enforcement officer."

Jonas decided that Kayo deserved better, so he told him about the village and the explosions. Kayo kept his mouth shut while Jonas explained, and then he rubbed his bald head where the hair used to be and said, "I'm glad you're seeing that fellow in Waylonsville. I'm glad to handle the phones and the radio while you go over there every Tuesday morning. I hope he can help."

"He's trying," Jonas said.

"I'll tell you this, Jonas, I have got to have someone here in the office that's stable. Tilda was a pain in the ass sometimes, but I could always count on her being stable. That last night..." Kayo seemed to run out of words and he looked at Jonas for a while and then got up and rattled around his office for a while longer and then left for Dairy Queen.

NINE

About four in the afternoon, Jonas at the console with the radios and phones, dispatching Milo to a convenience store where Mr. Patel, the owner, was refusing to let a guy from the fire department conduct an inspection after a fire in an air conditioning unit. Jonas knew from personal experience that Mr. Patel sold beer to minors, but what else?

He heard someone walk in, but he was occupied with the radio and didn't turn around. "Roger, Car Two. Let me know if you need backup." And that, he thought, was a joke because Car Two was the only car on duty. Car One was Kayo's, and Kayo — good man that he was — was pretty non-confrontational, and not likely to be keen for backup.

"I want to file a complaint," she said, and he turned and looked up at her, standing there in front of his desk with her arms folded and an odd look on her face. It had been two weeks since he changed her tire in the downpour, and then sprung her from jail. He had thought about her several times, but decided it wasn't worth the bother because he would never see her again. He was taken aback. After a moment he said, "What are you complaining about?"

"Oh," she waved her arms, "stuff in general."

"I don't think we have a category for that."

"You should. I'm all the time around people bitching and moaning about shit, and there ought to be a category called Stuff in General."

"Pull up a chair," he said, "and tell me about stuff. Why are you back here?"

She crossed the room, took hold of a heavy wooden chair, and made a show of scraping it loudly across the floor to him. She sat, crossed her legs, and gave him a long look. She was a lot better looking than he remembered. She had on a little tank top type thing and some skin-tight jeans. He remembered a waitress at a bar in San Diego and his fellow corpsman-in-training who said, "Her jeans are so tight, when she farts she blows her shoes off." This woman's jeans were about like that, and she filled them out spectacularly. "I'm back here," she said, "because you're the only person in the past month that's been halfway nice to me. My car's shot and I have thirty-five cents in my pocket."

Jonas felt a stab of panic. *Another needy soul on my doorstep. I don't need the needy. I want all the needies to go away and leave me alone.* Then he remembered what Doc said: *You're a kind and generous person, even when it gets you in trouble.* Well, he didn't need, wouldn't even consider, any more trouble.

"What happened to that gig you were heading toward?"

"It was okay, and there were a couple of others, but then at the last place, the owner tried to molest me, and when I kicked him in the balls, he refused to pay me."

"Did you go to the police?"

"He's also the district attorney."

"Oh."

"So here I am." She gave him a half smile, uncrossed her legs, re-crossed them, waited.

"I already fixed your flat and got you out of jail."

She made a face. "Big friggin' deal."

"So?"

"I need a place to crash for a few days until I can find a job and make some money and get the hell out of this pissant town."

Jonas held up his hands. "Look, there's a Salvation Army thing in Waylonsville. They'll help you."

"I told you," she said impatiently, "my car's shot. It barely made it here, and there's no way it will make it to Wigglesburg…"

"Waylonsville."

"…Whatever. I'm broke, I can't afford a motel. So you…" she smiled.

He studied her, heart sinking. Angular face framed by hair a color that made "brown" inadequate, pert nose, dimple. And those jeans. When she crossed and uncrossed her legs, he felt more than mildly stimulated. Also, she had that attitude: confident, direct, brassy. There was something else behind the exterior, but he couldn't quite figure out what it was.

. "Look, if you can't, or won't, I get it. Just thought I'd give it a shot. You were nice to me that one time, I thought you might be nice again." She paused for a moment, studied her fingernails while Jonas thought, *Is she flirting with me?* "I take it you're local, lived here all your life, know everybody and everybody knows you. I don't want to ruin your reputation or anything. A loose woman…they might drum you out of the Baptist Church."

"I don't belong to the Baptist Church. I don't belong to any church." He thought about Gladys at the Presbyterian. *Gladly the cross I'd bear.* "Are you loose?"

"No. Ask the asshole who tried to screw me." She gave him another long look, then gave a shrug and a sigh and stood, scraped the chair back across the room, and walked out.

He caught her on the sidewalk, staring at the old wreck of a car. "Hey, I don't even know your name."

"What does it matter?"

I have a couch," he said.

She smiled. When she let herself, she had a really nice smile. "Lyric," she said.

The engine gave a death rattle when he tried to crank it. How had she managed to get the thing, on its last legs, just far enough to die in front of the police station? "You can't leave it here," he said. "It's a no-parking zone. Kayo will have it towed."

"Who's Kayo?"

"My boss. The police chief."

"So what are we gonna do with it? It ain't gonna go on its own."

"We?"

He went back inside and got on the radio with Kayo, who was just leaving Dairy Queen after his afternoon snack. "Kayo, there's a car parked in front of the station, an old Nissan, won't run. Could you get Tuttle to tow it to his place?"

"Whose car is it, Jonas?"

"A young woman."

A long silence. "Is this a young woman of your acquaintance?"

"You could say so, yes sir. She's pretty much down on her luck. The car's dead. I'm gonna…" *What?* "…help her out a little, I guess. Look, I'll send her over to Tuttle's tomorrow and see what he can do to get it going."

"And in the meantime?"

"See if I can find her a place to stay the night," he lied.

Tuttle was there in fifteen minutes. Jonas had walked to work that morning, so he and Lyric rode with Tuttle to the bungalow and took her stuff out of the car before Tuttle headed on to the garage with it. He put her duffel bag and guitar case in the second bedroom, which had no bed, just some odds and ends of furniture and a couple of boxes of the stuff he had brought from his mother's. When he got back to the living room she was nosing around, looking over things, looking like she was…what? *Nesting? Hell, no.* "The couch," he pointed.

"Yeah, that's definitely a couch. It is a kinda short couch. Not so short as a love seat, but short, for sure."

"You know," he said, "you have one of the most sarcastic mouths I have ever seen or heard on a person." *Well, there were the Marines….*

"Wicked," she said. "I use it as a weapon. You would be surprised how many people will do what you want when you shoot 'em full of sarcasm, make 'em squirm."

"So, it's a short couch."

"And I am not a short person."

"Take it or leave it," he said.

She turned up her nose. "Damn, sarcasm fails again."

He took her to Dairy Queen. She devoured a hamburger, a large order of fries, and a chocolate shake. He wondered how long it had been since she had eaten. When she was finished she said, "You want my thirty-five cents?"

"Of course not. Lyric…that's your real name?"

"It is now. I had it changed when I decided to be a singer."

"What was it before?"

"Frances. People called me Franny."

"Where are you from?"

"What is this, Forty Questions?"

"Just trying to find out who you are. After all, you're sleeping on my couch."

"Do you think I'm sinister?"

"A little. But the Sheriff said he ran an ID check on you, and you don't have a criminal record."

"But then there was Franny..."

"Was she sinister?"

"Maybe a little. Do you sleep with a pistol under your pillow?"

"I don't have a pistol," he said. "I don't like guns."

"But you're a cop...well, sort of."

"My only weapons are a telephone and a radio. They don't shoot very well."

She took a last slurp from her milkshake and set the cup aside. "You know, you're pretty sarcastic yourself."

He was surprised. "Really? I never thought of myself that way."

"Well, you are. Is yours a weapon...or a defensive mechanism?"

"I don't know."

"Well," she said, "it sits better on you than it does on me. Thanks for the burger and stuff."

"You can pay me back when you find work. Is there anything you do besides sing? I don't know of any place in Copernicus that hires singers. All of the choir members at the Baptist Church are volunteers."

She thrust her arms skyward, laced her fingers, and bent so far to the left that she almost touched the window glass. "I'm a certified yoga instructor."

"I don't know anybody in Copernicus who does yoga, either."

She lowered her arms, put her hands flat on the table. "Maybe I'll start a trend, have this place so flexible they'll change the name to Spaghettiville."

They sat for awhile in silence while Jonas finished his bacon cheeseburger and soda. When he looked up she was staring out the window, but she didn't look as if she was really seeing anything. And she looked, for the first time, weary, as if she had let go of some of her fierceness. She looked almost…well, vulnerable. And that surprised him, because up to now she had mostly just shown her curtain of chin-jutting hardness and sarcasm, working hard to keep her distance, maybe just to keep it all together. He thought how it must be for her, out on the road by herself with a piece-of-shit car, a guitar, thirty-five cents, and assholes trying to get in her pants.

She turned back, saw him looking. "What?"

"Sorry you've had such a tough time." She shrugged, and he suddenly wanted to reach across the table and take her hand, but he held back. Instead, he said, "You need a good night's sleep."

The curtain came back down with a thump, the chin jutted. "Don't you fucking *dare* feel sorry for me."

They watched a few innings of a baseball game on TV (she was a Cubs fan) and then while she used the bathroom, he brought sheets and a blanket, extras Gladys had given him. "Anything else?" he asked as she spread them out on the couch.

"No, I'll just pretzel myself on this short couch and dream of a sold-out crowd at my Madison Square Garden concert."

"You're welcome," Jonas said.

She gave a little twist of her mouth and then said, "Thanks. I really mean it."

"You know," he said, "I often get myself in trouble when I help people."

"I'm not gonna be any trouble."

"We'll see," he said.

He closed his bedroom door, took off his clothes, and went to bed.

He was dreaming, and it was the same dream from the flight to Ramstein, when he was all busted up: the high school dance, the girl just out of reach, the ache of longing, the crushing sadness of it all. But this time, at the end, there was something different. The girl didn't disappear. She was right there, smiling. She touched his face. It was cool, gentle, soothing. He cried with gratitude, reaching for her, holding on, afraid to let go. And then the girl in the dream became the girl with the guitar, and he came to the slow realization that it was her, really and truly. She was hovering over him, hands moving, touching every part of his body, awakening flesh and soul. Hands, mouth. Harder than he had ever been in his life. Then slipping him into her, so deep there might not be an end to it. He rose to meet her, the two of them giving, receiving. Whimpers, then crying out like wild birds, high and shrill. She came, he came so hard he thought he might never have to come again. She touched hidden places, parts that he had lost and thought he might never find again. And he fell headlong into her.

She was wearing one of his old tee shirts — COPERNICUS HIGH GOLF — when she brought coffee. It didn't cover much. He was naked, hard. She looked him over, smiled. "Save it," she said. He tried to smile back, but it was pretty early for that. He had never been smiley or talkative in the morning. He pulled the sheet over his hardness and wished for a moment that she would go away and let him drink his coffee and go soft again and think about this. Instead, she sat on the edge of the bed. "Is it okay?"

He took another sip. "I don't use much sugar. But...yeah."

"I don't mean the coffee."

"Oh." He looked past her to the window, open to the back yard. Everything all green now, sound and smell of summer. He turned back to her. "I..." But he hadn't the foggiest notion what to say. Finally he said, "It's been a long time." *In a former life*, he thought. There had been the girl on the golf team in high school — just once, because she wanted to know what it was like — and a couple of times in San Diego before he shipped out, girls he met in bars off base, feeling faintly guilty afterwards, but also surprised at himself because he thought he was not very good with girls.

"I don't sleep around," she said.

"Neither do I."

She watched him for a moment. "I was lonesome," she said.

"I guess I was too." Another sip of coffee. "But...it was

nice."

She rose. "I've got to go find a place and a job."

She waited until he finally said, "You could stay here."

"Are you sure?"

He shrugged. "If you want to. Until you get..." *What?*

"Uh-huh." And she was gone, leaving him thinking, *Why am I doing this? The same old mistake? Or something worse?*

She was there just after two, carrying her guitar case, a take-out box, and a Styrofoam cup with a straw in the lid. She put the guitar case aside and set the box and drink on his desk. He looked up at her, questioning. "Well, open it. Merry Christmas."

Veal parmigiana, fried okra, a dollop of mashes potatoes, still warm. The drink, iced tea with plenty of sugar. "Where did you get this?"

Before she answered, she dragged the chair across the room to his desk and sat. "There was this little old woman coming out of Poulos's Café. I mugged her and took her stuff."

He started to laugh, but then he thought, *She might just be capable of it.*

He pointed at the food and drink. "You didn't get all of this for thirty-five cents."

"I got a job," she said, and looked smug.

"Where?"

"Poulos's Café."

She had walked in at mid-morning, she said, with her guitar case. Poulos was in a tizzy. His lone waitress, an elderly woman Jonas remembered from his youth, had won a big pot of money at the American Legion Bingo game last night, passed out from the shock, and cracked her head on a table. She would be out for awhile. Well, Lyric said she was really super at waiting tables, and could she help? She thought Poulos might prostrate himself and kiss her feet. She helped him with the lunch crowd and was going back for dinner. This, the stuff in the take-out box, was partial payment for the morning's work, payback for the Dairy Queen meal Jonas had bought last evening.

She had brought an extra set of plastic dinnerware and they

shared it at his desk while he handled the radio and phones. He was hungry. He wasn't a breakfast person.

"Eight bucks an hour plus tips," she said. "And not only that…tah-dah!…I'm singing on Thursday night."

"At Poulos's?"

"Well, it ain't Carnegie Hall, but you gotta start somewhere."

"Damn," he said. Then, "Do you can the sarcasm when you wait tables?"

"I try."

My God, he thought, *she is…hell, I don't know what she is. But whatever she is, I've never seen anything remotely like her. I am not up to this. Am I?*

When he finished work at five, he went to Tuttle's to see about her car. Bald tires ("Never pass inspection, Tuttle said), worn-out shocks, leak in the radiator, HVAC needed overhaul, starter on its last legs, battery ka-put. But the worst part, the transmission was shot. "How much?" Jonas asked.

Tuttle scratched his head, then his crotch. "Three, four thousand, probably. For everything. And that's if I could find a used transmission. And if the catalytic converter is still okay. Ain't had time to check that. Ask me, it ain't worth puttin' a wrench on it."

Jonas gave a silent groan. How long would it take her to make enough money to buy a car? And then that thing about her that made him tingle stirred a little and his insides went smiley. *It might take awhile. Enough of awhile for me to act like a fool, because that woman can probably make a fool out of any man she chooses to.*

"The girl," Tuttle said, "she's a friend of yours?"

"A recent acquaintance."

"Well," Tuttle's hand went to his crotch again, "she's a look-er."

"Oh," Jonas said, "you don't know the half of it."

He found Doc in the back yard beside his koi pond, deep in an Adirondack chair with a book. Doc slipped a book mark between the pages, closed the book, held it up. "Copernicus," he said.

"Somebody wrote a book about Copernicus? There's nothing here to write about."

"Not the town, the person."

"What about him?"

"Math and astronomy guy. Came up with the idea that the solar system revolves around the sun, not the earth. In 1543, that was a damned radical notion. He caught a lot of heat for it. Folks didn't like being told they weren't the center of existence."

"I'll bet."

"And guess who the fiercest critics were."

Jonas thought for a moment. "Religious types."

"Absolutely. They said his nutty idea contradicted the Bible, and they used the battle of Gideon as an example. The Hebrews were winning, but night was coming and it appeared the enemy would escape in the darkness. So Joshua prayed and the sun and moon stood still. They said that proved that the earth was the center of the universe, and it was held upright by God's hand. So that made this guy Copernicus a heretic."

"But Copernicus was right and the Bible was wrong."

"What if they were both right? The earth is not the center of the universe, but the story of the battle of Gideon is allegory. Whether the sun and moon actually stopped isn't the point. The point is that Joshua and his army kicked ass with God's help."

"What about the people who say the Bible is literally true?"

Doc smiled. "I guess that's what works for them. Just don't ever let 'em get hold of NASA." He paused. "Now, you know how this town got named for Copernicus?"

"No."

"They didn't teach you that in elementary school?"

"No."

"And you went all the way through Copernicus High School without learning about Copernicus?"

"It just never came up."

Doc pondered for a moment. "I guess that says a lot about the place." He laid the book aside. "Drawn out of a hat," he said. "It was originally Stewartsville, named for a family of Stewarts who came down from Massachusetts in the 1850's to start a grist mill, led by an ornery cuss named Gabe. When the Civil War broke out,

Gabe said, 'You people are stupid,' and moved the whole family back to Massachusetts. That pissed off the locals, so they decided to rename the place. They couldn't agree on anything, so they finally settled on drawing a name out of a hat. One fellow had been reading about Copernicus and that's what he put in the hat."

"Okay."

Doc gave him a quizzical look. "Do you discern any parallels here?"

"I'm searching," Jonas said.

"They did away with the name of a fellow who went against the grain, and named it for a fellow who went against the grain."

Jonas smiled. "Is that what you call irony?"

"A significant gap in your personal cultural development and the local educational system in general. Every person who lives here should be required to know about Copernicus. It might make them less hide-bound and provincial. Might shake them loose from the idea that Copernicus is the center of the universe. Make them get outside of themselves."

Jonas frowned. "Have you been talking to Lieutenant?"

"About what?"

"He said I'm hiding from myself. He said I need to climb out of my foxhole."

"Lieutenant's pretty perceptive. Did he offer any suggestions?"

"Rotary Club."

"That might be good," Doc said. "Although I don't quite see you as a Rotarian. Maybe Jaycees. Although, come to think of it, I believe the Jaycees disbanded a few years ago."

Jonas looked at his watch. Six.

"Going somewhere?"

Jonas told him about the kid, Ben, about the golf.

"That might qualify for climbing out of your foxhole."

"Yeah."

"Things okay at the house? Got everything you need?"

"Mom brought over some kitchen stuff." He thought instantly of the girl, bringing coffee in a too-short tee-shirt and felt a stir. "Just wanted to let you know," he said, "I've got a..." *What? Roommate? Girlfriend? Piece of ass?* "...somebody staying with me for a few days."

"The one who's helping out at Poulos's?"

"God, Doc."

"Nothing stays out of sight for very long in Copernicus, Jonas. When you think the place where you live is the center of the universe, it gives the gossip the patina of brilliance."

"Well…is it…"

"It's your house, Jonas. Rent's the same if it's just you or a tribe of Hutus."

As he headed toward his car he thought, *A tribe of Hutus might be simpler.*

Ben was waiting for him on the range. "You're late," he said.

"Not much."

"What really happened to your hand? I told Lieutenant what you said about the bar fight. He said ask you."

Jonas held up the hand. "Hunting accident."

"No it wasn't."

"Okay. I got shot. And that's all I'm gonna say about it, so don't ask."

Ben shrugged. "Okay."

"What else did Lieutenant say about me?"

"He said you quit the golf team. I told him what you said about being the best golfer that ever came out of Copernicus High, and he said that was right. He said you coulda gotten a college schol-arship, but you quit."

"Did he say why?"

"No, he said ask you. So, why?"

"It had nothing to do with golf. And that's all I'm gonna say about *that*. Now, do you want to work on your golf game, or should we go to the pro shop and see what psychoanalytical bullshit you and Lieutenant can come up with?"

"Psycho…what?"

"Never mind. Did you practice what we worked on yester-day?"

"Yeah."

"A lot?"

"I stayed up late," Ben said.

"Just the setup."

"Uh-huh."

"Did you swing a club?"

"Of course. You didn't think I wasn't gonna swing, did you?"

"Of course not." He plucked a club out of Ben's bag, handed it to him. "So, swing."

They stayed at it for a half-hour until Jonas said, "Okay, that's it."

"You still don't want me to hit a ball?"

"You're not ready."

"When am I gonna be ready?"

"When I say so."

Ben put the club away, reached in a pocket of his shorts, and pulled out a ten. "Oscar gave me some money," he said, thrusting it toward Jonas.

Jonas waved him off. "Save it. When I start letting you hit balls, that's when the big bucks start. I'll run a tab."

"I don't want nothing for free," Ben said. His face flamed, his jaw went rigid. "I don't need free shit from nobody. You ain't gonna let me pay, then fuck you."

"Hey," Jonas said gently, "easy. Like I said, we'll work something out." He reached to touch Ben's shoulder, but the kid flinched, turned away. Jonas gave him a moment. "Ben, we gotta get something straight. I offered to help, and you said okay. Any time you want to change your mind, that's all right by me. But my help doesn't include listening to you say 'fuck you.' You either clean up your mouth or we'll just forget it. Are we clear?"

"Yeah, I guess."

"Don't guess.'

"All right."

"Good. Now, give you a ride?"

"No." He jammed the money back in his pocket. "I don't need a ride." He snatched up his bag and stalked away toward the pro shop where his bicycle was leaning against the wall. Then he stopped and turned around and came back, the anger gone now.

"Mom said I shouldn't hitch rides," he said.

"Could I talk to your Mom? Make it okay?"

"No," Ben said. "You can't talk to my Mom."

"Why not?"

"She don't like you."

"Did she say why?"

"No."

"Did she tell you to stay away from me?"

"I don't care what she says."

"I don't want to get you in trouble," Jonas said.

Ben laughed, but there wasn't a shred of mirth in it. "Trouble? You don't know shit about trouble."

Jonas didn't say a word. He just held up his left hand. Ben stared at it for a moment, and then walked away.

TEN

The figures were back, or at least he thought they were. It was hard to tell. Something at the corner of his eye, but when he glanced that way, there was nothing.

Driving back to the house after a day at the police station, looking left at an intersection and *seeing them — not plainly, just a suggestion of figures, clustered together, everything faded at the edges. But now they were moving, out into the street.* He panicked, slammed on the brakes. A screech of tires right behind him, horn blasting. He looked in his rear view mirror, a car nearly in his trunk. He sat there. Another blast of horn and then the car tore around him, the guy at the wheel giving him an enraged finger. When he looked left again, whatever had been there was gone. He realized that his foot was jammed hard on the brake. He lifted it, the car edged on its own across the intersection, bumping on the curb. He put it in park, killed the engine, sat slack-mouthed, spooked, trembling for several minutes until he finally got it together enough to get moving.

And again. End of a day, running the ball retriever for Lieutenant on the driving range. Not much light left as he got closer to the trees at the end of the range. *And then there they were for sure — vague but unmistakable human shapes in the deepening shadows under the trees.* He stopped the machine, stared hard, trying to make out details. *No faces, but of course he knew who they were. They were still for a while. Waiting. But why? Then they began to move about and he thought they might leave the shadows and come for him. He screamed, "What do you want from me?" It stopped them. And after an agonizing moment they backed away, fading into the shadows until there was nothing but shadow left.*

He turned off the machine, stumbled out, sat hard on the grass, knees clutched to his chest, feeling his heart racing so fast he thought it might burst through his skin, taking body and soul with it.

Then Lieutenant's voice calling out from the other end of

the range, up by the mats and the gazebo. "Jonas...you okay?" Figures at one end, Lieutenant at the other. Slumped here, caught in the middle. *Am I supposed to choose? Or do I just get ripped apart and you each get half?*

Lieutenant was waiting for him, giving him a hard look. "I heard you yelling out there." Jonas opened his mouth, but nothing came out. "You look like something just scared the hell out of you."

"It did," he managed.

"What?"

"I can't..."

Lieutenant put a hand on his shoulder. His voice was soft now. "I've seen some things out there too. I decided to let them stay out there. You do the same."

* * * * *

When they made love, it was in the dark, as he wanted. No questions, just the coming together, place and time of refuge. She was more experienced, taught him things, took him by the body and led him into the cool, dark cave of her, and for a moment he could feel both sheltered and altered.

In the giving and taking, he came to the larger realization of her. In her giving and taking she revealed something deep and honest there in the dark — something vulnerable, bordering on shyness. She was easy with him. They were easy with each other.

For a time, there wasn't much talk, and that was okay. She left early for work, came in late. Long hours, saving her money. So they made love in the dark, and the rest, the things that were encroaching on him more by the day, stayed at arm's length.

But her fingers explored, and one night, when they were spent and floating from the sex, she turned on the bedside lamp. "Don't," he said, but her fingers were already on him, tracing the scars on his shoulder and thigh. Then she surprised him by saying, "I don't care."

"Don't care what?"

"Whether you tell me or not."

He started to say something dismissive, but then he thought, *What do I owe here? In return for honesty?* So he told her a little about

Afghanistan — what he knew of it, but not what he was beginning to suspect. Not the figures at the edge of his consciousness, not the growing sense of dread about what they meant and what he might do about them. "I got hit a couple of times," he said. "But I don't remember it."

"Does it hurt?"

"Sometimes. And there's the limp. But I'm okay."

And then he told her about Carl.

"Do you have PTSD?" she asked.

His guard went up, "What do you know about PTSD?"

"My old man." She told him about growing up in Louisiana, her mother moving out, fed up with things, her father a hand on an oil rig in the Gulf, long absences while she fended for herself. The oil rig blew up and he was burned. Unable to work, in pain a lot, nightmares. Finally drank himself to death. "I think he had PTSD. The booze let him try to hide from it." So she hit the road. She had a guitar and she could sing, and she did okay until the car broke down and she had thirty-five cents in her pocket.

"So this Carl. Does he help?"

"He tries. I hope…"

"What?"

"I guess…that he doesn't give up on me."

She turned off the light and they were quiet and he was beginning to doze off when she said, "Okay, that's it."

"That's what?"

"I've told all I'm gonna tell, and I think you've told all you're gonna tell. So we are who we are. Okay to leave it at that?"

"Yeah. I don't need another shrink."

"Good. 'Cause I ain't one. Except…I might put some of your shit in a song. I sure do put a lot of mine in 'em."

She sang Thursday nights at Poulos's. He went, sat at the back next to the door to the kitchen. Poulos had concocted some sort of a small stage where she sat on a bar stool. Just her and the guitar and a cheap sound system, a mic on a stand and an amp on the side. She had a strong, assured voice that made him think of a deep, pure stream, water tumbling gently over smooth rocks. She was good with the guitar, too — chords and riffs in an easy undercurrent for the words.

There was a nice crowd, mostly young. Poulos was hopping about, serving food and beer, looking happy. Most of his trade was at lunch, little old ladies who paid for their meat-and-threes by the week, along with folks who worked downtown.

Lyric bantered easily with the audience, did a few requests, covers of some Allison Krauss and Emmylou Harris. But it was mostly her own songs, things about people bumping up against each other and making connections — or not. The kinds of things that would resonate with a young crowd, the kinds that made them sit still and listen.

Hearing her, Jonas realized how much he missed music, listening to good, honest words and melodies. Realized it was one of the things he had kept at bay because a song, if it hit you just right (or wrong) could open up places you might not want to go. It wasn't just sad songs that made him cry. The toughest were the really pretty ones. He had tried for a good while not to go near places that made you cry. But here he was, sitting in Poulos's Café, letting her music in, and if his eyes started to leak, well it was pretty dim back in this corner. Right now, he was tired and empty, willing to let the words and chords ease into some of the hollow places and rest there without getting rowdy.

At the end of her set, after finishing a song with a little light run up the fretboard, she said, "You can stay here and drink all night if you want to, but this is last call for the music. This is one I wrote just today."

And she sang a song about somebody with baggage, toting it into a new relationship. The hook in the lyrics was, "I Ain't Babysittin' No Broken Heart."

That one made him cry, silent tears coursing down his cheeks. He slipped out through the kitchen and went home.

He was sitting in the dark when she came in, fumbling with the door, setting her guitar case aside, reaching for the light switch.

"The song tonight," he said, "I don't need a babysitter."

"That's good," she said, "because I heard enough whining self-pity from my father to last a lifetime. You start that, I'm on the road if I have to walk."

Babysitting Rodney. Gladys called, the Presbyterians needed her for something, so he went after work. Rodney in his wheelchair, parked in front of the TV set in the living room. A bass fishing tournament. Rodney had never been interested in fishing that he could remember. But maybe it didn't matter what was on TV.

"Hi," he said. Rodney nodded, his eyes following Jonas as he sat in what had been Rodney's recliner. Rodney still couldn't speak. But maybe that didn't matter, either. There were the home health people and Gladys and a catheter for when he needed to pee. The guy on TV, fishing from a sleek bass boat, outfitted in the latest Bass Pro Shops attire and gear, hooked a big large-mouth, fought him, reeled him in. Rodney grunted.

The dog, Pee Wee, trotted in, made a circle of the room, and made a sudden leap into Rodney's lap. Jonas expected him to take a swipe at the dog, but he just sat there, watching the bass boat guy. Jonas reached for the dog. It growled, he let it be. "Cute little fart, ain't he," Jonas said, then regretted it. *Rodney the dog-hater is defenseless. Don't be a shit. Leave it.* He wondered if he was beginning to feel sorry for Rodney, if maybe could leave at least some of the past where it belonged.

After a while, Rodney started making some guttural sounds, trying to twist around in the wheelchair. "Bathroom?" Jonas asked. Rodney nodded, screwing up his face even more than it was already screwed up. There was the catheter, but this must be the other. Jonas wheeled him down the hall to the bathroom, pulled his sweat pants and underwear down, helped him onto the commode, then left. It felt incredibly awkward, but he told himself it wasn't Rodney, just a sick old guy who couldn't do things for himself. Back in a few minutes, and Rodney nodded and grunted to let him know he was finished. Back in the chair, back in the living room — the TV doing an infomercial for a depth finder for your bass boat. And then Gladys was home.

She had a casserole in the oven, and after he helped her get Rodney to bed, they ate at the patio table. Still a good hour's light left. He thought of Lieutenant's place and then realized he had promised Ben he would be there after work. But here he was, babysitting Rodney. People needing him, not wanting people to need him. He began to feel something he thought might be a touch of panic at the back of his mind.

She prattled for a while about the Presbyterians — she was chairman of the church bazaar committee — and then she said, out of the blue, "You have a girl living with you."

Jonas concentrated on his plate. "She's not a girl, she's a young woman."

"Living with you."

"In my house," he said.

"I suppose you're having…" her voice trailed off.

He looked up. Her color was high, her voice rising. "That's none of your business, Mom."

"Don't you care what people think?"

"No. But I can tell you do."

"I certainly do," she flashed.

"Mom, I'm twenty-one years old, I've been to war, I can vote and legally drink alcohol, and if I want to have a live-in girlfriend… well, I have a live-in girlfriend. At least for now."

"People talk, Jonas."

"Let 'em."

"And you with a public position, working at the police department."

"So if I were breaking any laws, I'd be the first to know."

Gladys glared at him. "Jonas, you never used to be like this."

"What? My own person? No, I was always your son and Rodney's son. And you say people talk, didn't they talk when I was growing up and Rodney was riding my ass all the time and you let him?" He could feel his own face flushing hot now, the deep-down panic turning to anger.

He expected Gladys to lash out at him. Instead, she lowered her head, raised her hands to the table, set them softly on either side of her plate, and stared at them. "There are things you will never know," she said quietly. Then she got up and went to the kitchen and Jonas got up and went home.

Carl said, "You're carrying your childhood around on your back."

"I try not to think about it too much," Jonas said.

"But you do."

"When I'm over there at Mom's, around Dad…"

Carl studied his notepad for a moment. "Why do you think you could never please your father?"

"I guess by his standards, I didn't measure up," Jonas said. "He was a professional baseball player, great athlete. Byrd was a great athlete."

"Byrd?"

"My stepbrother. Good bit older than me, from Mom's first marriage. He was all-everything, played football at Auburn."

"Do you ever talk to Byrd about what it was like at home?"

Jonas shook his head. "Byrd and I never got along. He's twelve years older. I remember one time when I was about four and I walked into his room and he said, 'Get out. Come in here again and I'll fuck you up.' I never went in his room again."

"And now?"

"I haven't seen him in years. Have no idea where he is. He got hurt pretty bad playing football and just kinda disappeared."

"How did golf affect your relationship with your dad?"

"I thought it would make things okay." He stared at the floor for a moment before he said, "But it didn't."

* * * * *

When he was fourteen he tried out for the high school golf team. The coach watched him hit balls for five minutes and gave him a spot. As a freshman, he was already the best player, and he kept getting better. He spent most of his practice time at Lieutenant's place, but played rounds at the country club, always by himself, early morning, late afternoon when there wasn't much of anybody on the course. The golf, the sweet realization that he was really, really good at something, was a thing quietly his own.

Rodney was busy with baseball and didn't pay much attention. But one Friday at breakfast, he said to Jonas, "I've got us a 9:00 tee time tomorrow."

Jonas dropped his spoon in his cereal bowl, splashing milk. "Us?"

"You and me. Your coach, guys who see you at the range, they say you're pretty good. So I wanna see for myself."

He was a wreck — knees week, stomach churning, fumble-fingered, dropping things, barely able to get his bag on the back of the cart. It was a priceless Spring day — warm but not hot, a slight breeze, clear sky mottled by a few puffy clouds. But Jonas didn't notice until much later in the day.

It was just the two of them. First tee, an easy par four. Jonas managed to get a tee in the ground, the ball on top of it. He made a couple of tentative practice swings with his driver, then stepped up to the ball. He took a couple of deep breaths, trying to calm himself, trying to remember all that he and Lieutenant had worked on. But he was a complete blank. He swung — too quick, arms and hands and body going places they shouldn't, and hit a screaming hook into the woods on the left side of the fairway. He picked up his tee, stepped away, didn't look at Rodney, who teed up his ball, aimed left, and hit his usual slice. Middle of the fairway, two hundred twenty-five yards.

They found the ball with no problem, but there were trees in the way. The smart thing would be to just pitch it out into the fairway, but Jonas took aim at a narrow space between two trees and hit one of them squarely. The ball ricocheted back and landed at his feet. He felt close to tears. This time, he pitched it out. Still a long way from the green. He pulled out his three-wood, ripped at the ball, topped it. Another hundred yards closer. He glanced at Rodney, who stepped up and lashed a seven-iron to within thirty feet of the pin, then looked over at Jonas and smiled.

"Good spot…I mean good shot," Jonas croaked.

Four strokes later, Jonas managed to coax his ball into the hole. A quadruple bogey. Rodney had a par. "Not your best effort," Rodney said with a smirk. And that's when Jonas got mad.

"Never play angry," Lieutenant had told him, and he thought about that, then thought, *screw it*. Instead, he remem-

bered what else Lieutenant had said: "Knock the piss out of it."
He stepped up to his ball on the second tee, a longish par five, in a
cold fury that somehow calmed him. All the Lieutenant stuff came
back. He settled into his stance, took a long, slow back swing, and
then exploded into the ball. It blasted off the tee, kept climbing and
climbing, reached a beautiful apex, fell to the fairway, bounced and
rolled and kept on rolling. Two hundred fifty yards if it was a foot.
He held his follow-through then relaxed, lowered the club, picked up
his tee, and started toward the cart. He didn't look at Rodney this
time either, but he thought, *Where's your smirk now, asshole?*

But Rodney surprised him. "That was one helluva golf
shot," he said softly.

Jonas looked. There was a gleam in Rodney's eye, the kind
he had only seen when Rodney talked about his baseball team. Or
before that, when Byrd was playing at Auburn. "Thanks," he said.
They played the rest of the round in what Jonas thought was, amaz-
ingly, something akin to camaraderie. He shot a seventy-eight, even
with the quad bogey. When they got home Rodney said to Gladys,
"I think we've got a real golfer here." Jonas's young heart sang. He
wanted to run around the house and yard screaming with joy. Instead, he went to his room and just savored and smiled. A lot.

And then there was Fred Wesley. "You like this golf stuff,"
Fred Wesley said.

"Yes I do. A lot."

"Do you need one of those guys that totes the bag around?"

"A caddy."

"Yeah."

"I sure do."

Fred Wesley didn't know much about golf, but the thing
about Fred Wesley was, he was able to focus on something better
than anybody Jonas had ever known. It was just part of the way his
mind worked — never fast, but tenacious. They went out to Lieutenant's place and Jonas talked him through the bag, all the clubs
and what they were for, when and where Jonas hit them. Then he hit
balls while Fred Wesley watched silently, standing there with hands
on hips, taking it all in. Finally they got a pencil and paper and Jonas
wrote down all the clubs and the yardages for each one. "Got it?"
Jonas asked when they were finished.

"Yep. I'm slow but…"

"Right."

"You want to try to hit a few balls, Fred Wesley?"

"Nope."

"You might be good at it."

Fred Wesley smiled. "I'd rather just watch you be good at it."

Next, they went to the country club and Jonas played a round and explained all about par-threes and par-fours and par-fives and greens and bunkers and the rules of golf. He wrote that all down. They sat on the patio behind the clubhouse drinking sodas while Fred Wesley pored over all the notes, his brow furrowed. Then Fred Wesley looked up and smiled. "I can do that."

In Jonas's junior year, Fred Wesley caddied for him at every match. Most of the players just carried their own bags, but caddies were okay and Fred Wesley became a fixture at the tournaments. Here, he was just another guy who liked golf. Jonas discovered to his delight that Fred Wesley was a whiz at reading greens. He could see things Jonas couldn't. He would lean over Jonas's shoulder as he lined up a putt, mutter a word or two, never point, and be uncannily dead on. Jonas's putting improved.

But mostly, Fred Wesley kept him loose. They chatted as they marched down fairways, mostly about everything except golf, Jonas marveling at Fred Wesley's slightly skewed way of looking at things. One afternoon as the golf team was playing a practice round at the country club, Jonas hit an approach into a bunker with a high lip, and when they got there, the ball was nowhere to be seen.

"Buried," Jonas said with dismay.

"No," Fred Wesley said, "a wild golf got it?"

"A what?"

"Wild golf. It's a little animal. Sometimes they live under bunkers, and when a ball lands in there, the wild golf jumps up and grabs it and takes it down under the sand. And sometimes they live in the woods, and if you hit the ball near the woods, they'll run out and grab it and throw it in deep. And sometimes they live just under the greens, and when you putt, they'll hump up their backs and make a little bump in the green and the ball goes off line."

Jonas was speechless for a moment. "Fred Wesley, where did you hear that?"

Fred Wesley grinned. "I made it up."

After that, they made allowances for the wild golf factor, as Jonas called it. Don't land in bunkers or near the woods, and when you get to a green, stomp on the edge of it to scare off the wild golfs. Jonas never told anybody else about the wild golf factor, not because he thought it was silly or stupid, but because it belonged to just him and Fred Wesley.

By the time he was a senior, Jonas was considering scholarship offers — a couple of big schools, Georgia and South Carolina, and several smaller ones with good golf programs. He thought he might be more comfortable in a smaller place.

At home, there was a sort of truce, and Jonas realized that golf had done that. Rodney pretty much left him alone. He made it to a couple of Jonas's tournaments when the baseball team didn't have a game. He kept his distance, but at one of the tournaments, when Jonas had finished in first place by eight strokes, he offered a hand and they shook. It wasn't a hug — Rodney had never hugged him — but it was something.

In the middle of the season, the golf coach was injured in an automobile accident. Out for the rest of the year. So Rodney volunteered to coach golf. The baseball team was rebuilding, probably not a state playoff contender. He would be at all the practices, and if a game conflicted with a golf match, he would be with the baseball team. Besides, what the golf kids needed was just somebody to organize things, keep up with matches, make sure they got where they needed to be. And there was Jonas. Heck, Rodney said, Jonas was already as much a coach as the guy who held the title. So the principal said okay.

And then Rodney started coaching. He was full of tips and advice and rah-rah pep talks. The golfers looked at each other, rolled their eyes and made faces when Rodney wasn't looking, and looked to Jonas. But Jonas wasn't any help because Rodney was on his ass more than anyone's. They played a practice round at the country club, tuning up for the conference tournament, and Rodney followed Jonas every step of the way — correcting, needling, sniping. *That was too much club, Jonas. See, you're over the green in the rough. What's with all the practice swings? You're wearing me out. Just play the shot. Don't make stupid mistakes, Jonas. The rest of these guys and a bunch of college coaches are watching you. Be an example…Jonas…Jonas…Jonas…Jonas…*

But the worst part was that Rodney ordered him to stop using Fred Wesley. "None of the other guys have a caddy. It sets a bad example. Carry your own bag." Jonas protested vehemently, but Rodney was unyielding.

And so without Fred Wesley to keep him loose, and under Rodney's white-hot scrutiny, Jonas's game began to fall apart. It wasn't that he had forgotten what to do. Instead, when he approached a golf ball, he could feel the tension seizing him by the throat and gut, and he was powerless to stop it. He sweated, his stomach churned, his vision blurred. Within two weeks of Rodney taking over, Jonas was a wreck. They lost the conference tournament by six strokes to a team that wasn't nearly their equal in talent, and Jonas shot an 86, his worst round in four years of competition. At home that night, Rodney berated him. "You're supposed to be a leader, Jonas. You let your team down. Get your shit together, or those college coaches are gonna forget you."

The conference tournament was the team's only loss, so they qualified for state. Jonas prayed fervently that it would take place on the same day as a baseball game, but no such luck. Rodney drove the bus — two hours of sullen silence from the kids after he said sternly, "Get your game faces on." Jonas sat in the very rear, earbuds blasting Guns 'N Roses and Kenny Chesney, eyes closed, trying to rummage through the clutter that was his mind and soul and come up with some sort of way to get his shit together. He had had a good practice yesterday at Lieutenant's place. Lieutenant got him calmed down, showed him that the only thing wrong with his swing was "the six inches between your ears." And Fred Wesley had given him a pep talk.

The best high school golfers in the state were there, along with a flock of college coaches. Jonas started strong — two birdies, two pars on the first four holes. But then Rodney cranked up. Every time Jonas walked off a green, Rodney was there with a remark. Some of it sounded like he was trying to be helpful, but there was some snide criticism, too. And Jonas began to leak oil. A bogey, then a double.

On the seventh hole, Jonas hit a decent drive and lofted an 8-iron to the edge of the big, undulating green. He stood over the putt for a long moment, then made the mistake of looking up, seeing

Rodney standing a few yards off the green, arms folded, glaring. He silently mouthed, *Make it.* Jonas felt panic rising — knees weak, hands sweating. He took a deep breath, but that didn't help. So he went ahead and stroked the putt and left it twelve feet short. The second putt never had a chance, sliding by four feet. He managed to coax that one into the edge of the hole. A three-putt bogey. He stood, head down, at one side of the green while another kid in his foursome finished. He turned to walk off and there was Rodney, blocking his way, glaring, shaking his head in disgust.

They stood facing each other for a moment, Jonas hoping the earth might open and swallow him. When it didn't, he side-stepped Rodney and walked to his bag. There was a good crowd following the foursome — mostly coaches and parents. He didn't put the putter in the bag. Instead, he laid it gently on the grass beside it and walked off, heading toward the clubhouse.

"Hey!" Rodney yelled. "Pick up your bag!"

Jonas kept walking. Rodney was on him in a flash, grabbing his shoulder, spinning him around. "What in the hell do you think you're doing?"

"I quit," Jonas said, and felt an enormous flood of relief.

"You can't just…quit."

"Yes sir, I just did."

Rodney was bug-eyed and loud. The crowd had frozen, every eye on them. "Do you realize what you're doing? Quit in the middle of a round, the state tournament, no college coach in his right mind will give you the time of day."

Jonas kept his gaze locked on Rodney's face. "Dad," he said firmly, "you don't know shit about golf. You make it…not fun any more." He paused for a moment. "So go fuck yourself."

Rodney hit him in the stomach. Jonas felt all the air go out, doubled over and collapsed. The crowd was on them, pulling Rodney away, bending over Jonas, who lay there writhing and gasping and beginning to accept the pain, the most genuine thing besides a good golf shot he had felt in a long time. By the time they helped him to his feet Rodney was gone. Somebody got a cart and they took him back to the clubhouse. Two hours later, Doc was there.

Jonas was in his room, doing trigonometry homework, when

Rodney got home that evening. Jonas could hear him clomping down the hall, then he shoved open the door. Jonas didn't look up at him. *Sign and cosign. At least that made sense.*

"Get out," Rodney said, his voice all shards of wicked glass. "Get out of my house."

"It's not your house, it's Mom's house."

"But I decide who lives here. And you don't."

Jonas looked up now at Rodney filling the door. He was powerfully-built, the old fireballer, even now that he had gone soft around the middle. Jonas felt a hint of the fear with which he had lived for so long, the abiding sense of being at Rodney's mercy. But not now, he told himself. He had stepped across a threshold, left part of himself behind there beside the seventh green. "Yes sir," he said, rising and reaching for the jacket hanging on the back of his desk chair.

"You can stay tonight," Rodney said, "but I want your ass out of here in the morning."

"Thank you," Jonas said, as politely as he knew how.

He found Gladys in the living room, sitting quietly in an overstuffed chair, hands folded in her lap. "Why?" he asked. "Why did you let him do that?"

"I…" she choked, "…I can't tell you."

He turned away and went to bed. He skipped school the next day, found some boxes, started packing his stuff. There wasn't much — clothes, books, laptop, a few trophies, odds and ends. Then Doc came around noon and they put his stuff in Doc's Suburban and hauled it over to his place.

Rodney was suspended from the school faculty for the rest of the semester and he had to go before the school board and apologize. The board voted to uphold the suspension but allow him back in the Fall. The state high school athletic association issued a stern reprimand and put him on a year's probation. Jonas didn't see him again. There was no apology coming his way, and that was okay because he really didn't want one.

The week of final exams, he walked into a Navy recruiter's office and signed up.

Carl was scribbling. Jonas waited until he looked up. "I haven't picked up a golf club since."

"Why not?"

Jonas grunted. "Honest? I blame it on my hand, but I think it's just a matter of dredging up all that old shit."

"Did you let your father take golf away from you?"

"No, I did that all by myself."

Carl flipped to a fresh page in his notepad and scribbled for awhile. Then he laid the pad aside. "So, back to the beginning. Toting your childhood around with you."

"I guess I am. I argue with my Mom. She never had my back, and she won't tell me why. Was she just scared shitless of him, or was it something else?"

"Any guesses?"

"No."

"I was an English major before I switched to psychology," Carl said. "Read a lot of good books. One of my favorite authors was Saul Bellow. And I remember something he wrote in one of his novels where he said, in effect, you can't go around being a wounded child forever."

"Doc said the same damn thing," Jonas said hotly. "You think that's all I am? A wounded child? Children don't go where I've been."

Carl held up his hands. "Let's go at this a different way. You had a difficult childhood and youth. Feeling inadequate, trying hard to do everything right, protecting your mother. That's a pretty heavy load for a kid. But it doesn't stop there. You do carry your childhood with you. We all do. It echoes through the rest of our lives, good and bad. For you, it's an undercurrent to what you brought home from Afghanistan. And there's the stuff you took with you to Afghanistan."

"Like what?"

"You were a hands-on, help-people guy. Keeping people patched up and alive, as best you could. You did all that because of who you are, who you *have* to be."

"It sounds like a big, tangled-up shit-storm."

"If I were obsessed with diagnoses, I could give it a clinical name. Complex PTSD."

"Another name for big, tangled-up shit-storm."

"Here's an example," Carl said. "A woman is raped. Horrible experience. All the signs of PTSD: withdrawal, nightmares, so forth. But what if that same woman was abused in childhood?"

"Makes it worse," Jonas said. "I get it."

"So she isn't just a rape victim. She's a wounded child who was raped."

"Does that mean I'm totally fucked?"

"No, but it means a lot of different lines and angles. All connected. And that's how you see it and deal with it." Carl glanced at the clock on the wall behind Jonas. "Next week, we put everything on the table."

Jonas sat unmoving for a moment.

"Anything else?" Carl asked.

Jonas thought about telling him about the figures. At the edge of things, moving a hair closer each time, the growing insistence. Not ready to go there yet. Maybe next week, if they were going to put everything on the table. Then, "There's a woman."

Carl's eyebrows went up. "And?"

"She's staying with me until she gets a car. Well, I guess it's a little more than that."

"And how do you feel about that?"

Jonas tried a smile. "It's nice. But that's just part of it. She seems…I don't know…safe."

Carl smiled. "Reason enough."

ELEVEN

In the afternoon, after work, he went to Lieutenant's place looking for Ben. Lieutenant was sitting in the gazebo beside the practice range, wearing faded khaki shorts, drinking coffee from a NASCAR Hall of Fame mug. There was no sign of Ben.

"You seen the kid?"

"He was out here yesterday, looking for you."

"I was helping Mom. I forgot."

Lieutenant peered into his cup as if looking for clues to something. Then, "If you're gonna help him, do it. If you're gonna blow him off...for any reason...go ahead and tell him. Are you afraid he's gonna ask you to pick up a club?"

"He already did."

"And you said..."

"I can't."

"Well then, you're lying to yourself."

Jonas shook it off. "You got beer inside?"

"Fridge in the back. Bring me one."

Jonas came back with the two beers. "Where did you get the mug?"

"At the NASCAR Hall of Fame, where do you think?"

"You've been there?"

Lieutenant took a swig of beer and made a face at Jonas. "Duuhh."

"Ever been to a race?"

"Hell, no. Too much noise, too many drunks eating Kentucky Fried and throwing the bones at each other. I watch on TV. Does that surprise you?"

"Kinda."

"There was a black driver some years back. Wendell Scott. I met him once. Been following NASCAR ever since. Been a couple of others, but none like Wendell."

"Well, I'll be damned," Jonas said.

"Yeah," Lieutenant muttered. "You just be damned. Greedy white folks, trying to keep NASCAR to themselves."

They sat drinking their beers for a while and then Lieutenant said, "What have you figured out about the kid?"

Jonas gave him a long look. Lieutenant had a way of keeping things close when he wanted to, talking around the edges.

"I know he lives in a shit hole, he's pretty much pissed at the world. And he's scared of something. Maybe the low-life guy that's living there."

"Maybe," Lieutenant said.

"What do you know about him? What are you trying to tell me?"

"I ain't trying to *tell* you anything. I'm just askin'."

"Well," Jonas said, "I can't tell what you're getting at."

"You met the kid's mother?"

"No."

"He say anything about her?"

"Just that she doesn't like me and doesn't want him hitching rides with me."

"Why do you think she said that?"

"Shit, Lieutenant, I don't have the foggiest goddamn idea," he said, voice rising. "Maybe she's from one of those families that got fucked over when the plant closed. Maybe she doesn't like people who drive Hondas." He paused for a moment, glaring. "What do you think?"

Lieutenant shook his head. "Forget I said anything. I just see you working with the kid, and I couldn't get to first base with him. I offered, but he blew me off."

"He said he doesn't take lessons from you because he can't pay."

"Everybody pays, but I told him we could work something out."

"How about me, when I was out here all the time? I never paid."

Lieutenant shrugged. "Well, somebody did."

"Doc?"

"Could be."

"Is Doc your investor?"

"Was in the beginning. I paid him back every cent and then some. It's all mine now, but Doc has some scholarships. I offered one to Ben, but he said he doesn't take nothing from nobody."

"Have you talked to Doc about Ben?"

"Sure have, just the other day."

"And what did he say?"

"He said it's your deal."

Jonas set his beer aside. "Well, damn," he said, "seems you and Doc know more about me than I know myself."

Lieutenant nodded. "These days, you may be right."

"Well, I'm not gonna go there."

"Okay. What about the kid? You gonna keep helping him?"

"Since you know so much," Jonas said, "you tell me."

"Yeah, you are. Since I'm supposed to know you better than you know yourself, of course you are. You can't not. It's in your bones, Jonas."

"Do you have a phone number for Ben?"

"If there's a phone at the place, I'm pretty sure it ain't Ben's. Never seen him with one."

Jonas got up to go. "Put your empty in the recycling," Lieutenant said. And when he was halfway to the pro shop, "Sooner or later, you're gonna pick up a golf club. I bet Doc a lot of money on it."

Jonas just kept walking.

He went to Poulos's. She was there, bustling about. A good crowd, more than he remembered seeing in the evenings, and he wondered if Lyric had anything to do with it. It was a couple of days until Thursday, so no music, but she looked good with her hair sort of flopping around on her head and those tight jeans and a low-cut blouse. She didn't have a lot of clothes in that duffel bag, but what she had, she looked damn good in.

He thought about her in his life, in his bed. He had never had anyone in his bed, at least not for a whole night. When he was small, he would climb into Gladys and Rodney's bed when he had a bad dream or there was a storm outside, but that ended abruptly when he was about three. He remembered crawling in one night, terrified of the huge bird at his window, flapping its wings to get in. Rodney snatched him up and took him back to his room and dumped him in his bed. "Don't ever do that again," Rodney said.

"But the bird…"

"It's just a limb, Jonas. Grow up a little, huh?"

But now he had a woman in his bed every night and it was more than good. There was just the one thing nagging at the back of his mind. She wouldn't stay. And the longer she *did* stay, the closer it got to the time when he would have to go it…if not alone, then without what she had come to mean. The giving and taking. Another failure, another loss.

"Special is a bowl of clam chowder and a crab cake sandwich," she said, leaning across him to put silverware in a rolled-up napkin at his place.

"Clam chowder in the summer?"

"Yes, and it's damned good."

"On your recommendation…"

She was gone, back in a few minutes with the chowder and sandwich. "You got a minute?" He wanted more than anything in the world for her to sit down and keep him company.

Her arm swept the room. "Oh, I got all the time in the world, Jonas. After nine o'clock."

She bustled away. He ate, watching her work, thought about the stories of people going to Nashville or Hollywood, waiting tables, being discovered. She was pretty damned good with that guitar and that sturdy voice and the songs she wrote. Just light out and grab a piece of the world. He thought, I've got a car. Maybe one day just light out? Not Nashville or Hollywood though, nothing about Jonas Boulware to be discovered out there in the rest of the world. Right now, it was just all here. If he could stand it. *But maybe one day…*

He finished, left her a good tip at the table, paid the tab to Poulos at the cash register, and headed for Ben's.

It was almost dark when he got to the trailer. It looked more forlorn than ever — the weeds going riot in the summer heat, a tangle of old pieces of lumber added to the clutter. The place was all closed up. Quiet except for the drone of a small air conditioning unit at one of the windows. It had been in the high eighties today, and the heat still clung in the humid air. He sat behind the wheel of the Honda looking at it for a long time, feeling despair creep up his spine. He got out, climbed the rickety wooden steps, and knocked. Nothing. He tried again, banging harder, listening for any sound of life inside. Finally, he tried the handle, and to his surprise, the door swung open. The heat and smell rocked him back on his heels. Piss, shit, rot, decay. He gagged.

And then there was Ben, wearing a sagging, filthy pair of tighty-whities, arms locked across his skinny chest, shivering in the heat. "Ben!" he cried, and took a step toward the interior.

"Don't come in here!" Ben yelled. "Don't ever come here!"

"Are you..."

"I'm fine! Get the fuck out! Leave me alone!"

Jonas tried to keep his voice low. "Is there anybody else here? Your Mom? Is Oscar here?"

"There's nobody here!" Ben's voice broke, something close to a sob. But his face was hard with rage. And yes, terror.

And then Oscar's voice — harsh, guttural, slurred — from somewhere in the back of the trailer. "Shut the goddamn door, Ben. You're letting the heat out."

"Please," Ben said, low and quavering now. "Just go. If you don't..."

"What, Ben? What if I don't go?"

Ben shook his head mutely.

"Let me help," Jonas said. "Come with me. We'll get in the car and go to town and talk about this."

He thought for a moment Ben might do it, but then his shoulders slumped and his voice was full of quit. "There's nothing to talk about," Ben said.

"Ben, I'm sorry about missing our session. Really, truly sorry. I want to help. Golf, whatever. I know a little about what this..." he took in the trailer, the awfulness, with a jerk of his head, "...is like."

"No, you don't," Ben said. He moved toward the door, reached around Jonas for the handle, gave Jonas a hard push. "You don't know shit."

Jonas stood there for a moment, barring the way, but then he saw it was no use, and he stepped back and let Ben close the door with a slam that tore through his head like something blowing up. He sat heavily on the steps and stayed there for a long time until the sound faded, leaving only an echo.

He was shaking, and it took Doc and a Valium to get him calmed down enough to tell Doc about it. Doc listened while he spilled it all out, and then he said, "If you think the boy's in danger, we should tell Kayo."

"I don't know what's going on out there — with Ben, with that guy Oscar — but you can tell, he's scared," Jonas said.

Kayo was there in fifteen minutes and Jonas went through it again — calmer now, but with a growing sense of another failure. Kayo asked some questions, and then he said, "I know the place. We've been out there a few times — domestic stuff. The mother's a slut and there's a succession of men. Never seen any evidence of dope, but that don't mean it's not there. More than likely, it is."

"You gotta go get him," Jonas said. "Now."

Kayo shook his head. "It's not that easy, Jonas. I can't just go barging in and take the youngster."

"But he's in trouble," Jonas insisted, voice rising. "Anybody can see it."

"He may be."

"And you're just gonna leave him out there!" He was almost shouting now.

Doc put a calming hand on his shoulder. Jonas tried to shake it off, but Doc held on. "Jonas, Kayo is going to do his job. Kayo, tell Jonas what you're going to do."

"In the morning," Kayo said, "I'll go to Social Services and report what you've told me. And then I'll go out there to the trailer with a social worker and see what we can find. If we can't get in the trailer, I'll go back to town and get a search warrant. If things are as bad as you believe they are, Social Services can take custody of the kid. We'll get him out of there. We'll make sure he's safe."

"I'm sorry," Jonas said. "I didn't mean to…"

"You mean to help that youngster," Kayo said gently. "It's

what you do."

When Kayo was gone, he sat for awhile on the front porch with Doc. "The other day, when I was talking about Ben," Jonas said, "you said 'Be careful.' What did you mean?"

There wasn't much light on the porch, just a bit from the street light down the way, and Jonas couldn't read Doc's face. But there was something in his voice — wariness? Reluctance? "I delivered Ben Cameron fourteen years ago."

It hung there in the night air and it took Jonas awhile to frame words. "Then you know who his father is."

"On the birth certificate, it says 'Unknown.'"

"But you know." Doc was silent. "Who?"

"I can't say."

"Why?"

"Because I don't have the right."

"Why are you telling me this, or at least a little piece of this. Does it have something to do with me?"

Doc stood slowly, pushing himself up from the armrests of the rocker. "Jonas, go home and go to bed."

Jonas stayed seated. "Doc, you're chickenshit."

"Probably. More than probably. More than you could ever know."

Doc went inside, but Jonas stayed on the porch for awhile longer, mind roiling, heart in knots, before he gave up.

Lyric was waiting up for him. "Where have you been?"

He told her about Ben, the golf, the trailer, tonight, Kayo. "It sounds pretty rotten," she said. "But it doesn't sound like anything you can fix."

"I don't seem to be able to fix shit," he said.

"So you just beat yourself up over it."

He had no answer for that.

Kayo was gone for a good while, and when he came back to the station around lunchtime, he had a wry look on his face. He stood in front of the console where Jonas was working. "Jonas," he said, shaking his head, "there doesn't seem to be anything wrong out there."

"You don't believe me?"

"It's not that. It's just that…Ramona from Social Services went with me. No sign of the kid or of this guy Oscar. The kid's mom was there. Pleasant, cooperative, answered all our questions. Yes, there had been a man there, but she said he had left. The kid, Ben, was okay, was out at the golf place. The place is run-down, but fairly clean inside. So Ramona and I went out to Lieutenant's. The kid was there, but he wouldn't talk to us. Couldn't make him, of course. So…" he spread his hands.

Jonas was incredulous. "So that's it? You're gonna just leave Ben out there in that shithole?"

"There's nothing I can do, or Social Services, not at this point. We've got to have some evidence to step in. And there isn't any."

He found Ben at the range. Same ratty shorts and faded polo shirt. Defiant. "Leave me alone," he said.

"Ben, listen, if there's anything I can do…"

"If you're not gonna teach me how to swing a golf club, just get the hell away." He glared at Jonas for a moment, then reached in his bag and pulled out a club, thrust it toward Jonas. "Show me."

"I haven't touched a golf club in a long time," Jonas said.

"Put up or shut up."

Jonas looked away downrange, out toward the tree line that marked the outer boundary, three hundred yards away. Once upon a time, if he caught it just right, he could send a golf ball almost to the trees. He looked back at Ben, holding the club, looking fierce. *If I don't do it, I've lost him. Like I lost myself.* He took the club with his right hand, wrapped it around the grip. Heart racing, sweat popping out on his forehead, stomach knotting. Left hand on the club, three fingers, an enormous space where the others had been.

Ben watched him, unyielding, then took a ball out of the basket and placed it on the mat. "Hit the bastard," Ben said, his voice like ice.

Jonas took his stance at the mat. Ball at his feet, club face behind the ball. Start the back swing with the shoulders, hinge the wrists, slight pause at the top, then down and through, hips leading. Contact. Follow through as the ball rises, watching it downrange. Not far, not straight. But out there, out where his youth had once been, a long time ago when he was a wounded child. He felt ancient. Dropped the club, sat down heavily next to the mat, staring at his feet.

Then Lieutenant was there. Jonas looked up. Lieutenant didn't say a word. Just Ben, who said, "That's all I want from you. The rest, shove it up your ass."

* * * * *

He began to feel his old wounds. It wasn't much at first — tingle of nerve endings, twitch of muscle fiber, cramps in his leg and shoulder. He tried to ignore it, and mostly did until the tingling and twitching and cramping became sudden, sharp pains that shot from his hip all the way to his toes, and stabs in his upper back that felt like someone had plunged a hot poker into sinew. He could go a day or so with nothing, but then feel the shock of hurt that took his breath, woke him in the night, made him double over, groaning, until it passed.

"I heard you moaning again last night." Lyric said. "Nightmare?"

"Gas, probably."

"That wasn't a gas moan. If something's wrong, you need to tell Doc."

Doc checked him over, found nothing cockeyed. Still, there was the pain. "You were badly wounded and patched back together, "Doc said. "In a trauma like your body experienced, there's nerve damage, and then there's scar tissue as you heal."

"But it's been months, Doc."

"Nerves take time to regenerate. About a centimeter a week. The scar tissue…it can cause problems over time. You did rehab in the hospital."

"A lot," Jonas said.

"But since then, you've been pretty sedentary. Exercise? Walking? Golf?"

"Not much."

"So the broken places are still mending and the scar tissue continues to form and it causes problems. You've got to be more active. And God knows, you need to gain some weight. You look gaunt."

"Could it be…" he hesitated, "…in my head?"

Doc thought about that for awhile. "The pain is real, Jonas. But there's a psychological component to pain. How much? No absolute way of telling. Everybody's different."

"Can you give me something to help?"

"I could, but I won't. Not until you see the VA doctors. I don't have their kind of expertise in treating trauma. The Navy people, when they were putting you back together, found no evidence of TBI — traumatic brain injury — but maybe they missed something."

Jonas felt a stab of panic. "So my brain may be fucked up?"

"When you were wounded, was there an explosion?"

"Things blew up."

"When a powerful explosion happens, the brain can be bounced around inside the skull. It can bruise, and that can take time to heal. Or the damage can be lasting. As I said, the medical report didn't find any sign of it in your case. But it should be looked into again, along with anything else that may be the source of what you're feeling."

"Okay."

"Pain is both a negative and a positive, Jonas. We don't like to hurt, but hurt tells us something about our bodies and our souls. Pain insists on itself. It says, 'Pay Attention To *Me!*'" He stopped, waited a long moment. "Then, maybe it's something else, telling you it's time to climb out of the foxhole."

We've talked about this before," Carl said. "Reconnecting. One of the inevitable consequences of experiences like you've had is a feeling of being unconnected. From people, from places, from emotions. In your case, memory. You don't remember because if you did, it would be profoundly painful. So you invent a substitute life."

"The new normal," Jonas said.

"Exactly. You separate yourself from the painful things in

your life. So in a very real way, you're disconnected from yourself. And it sounds like yourself is insisting on being heard. So we look for ways to help the re-connecting. In your case, golf might be a good way. It was one of the good things in your life, even if it wasn't all good."

"But," Jonas said, "what if you dredge up the bad shit while you're doing it."

"The risk you have to take," Carl said. "The risk that in re-connecting with one compartment of your life, other things begin to open. Doors you've worked hard to keep shut. Memories. Bad stuff."

"What if I can't do that? Or won't"

"You don't have a choice," Carl said. "You already have."

* * * * *

It began to come back to him in pieces, and the first piece was Hinshaw.

It came suddenly in the night, the world exploding in sound and fury and madness, a thunderous force that lifted him and smashed him back to earth. Dust, smoke, fire, everything flying apart in pieces. Noise, blotting out everything. He struggled to rise, stumbled, went down, tried again, hurling himself forward. On his feet now, people screaming. Got to get to them. A step, two, three, his legs rubbery. And then he looked down and saw Hinshaw, or what was left of him. An arm gone, along with his lower jaw, a gaping hole where his stomach used to be, shreds of intestine, gore. Nothing left but the eyes. Hinshaw's eyes — wide, terrified, boring in on him. But there were the screams out there, people who needed him. Hinshaw wouldn't make it. Not enough left to cobble together. But Hinshaw needed him with his eyes. Jonas stared, horrified — not at Hinshaw, but at the knowledge that he couldn't stop, that he couldn't help Hinshaw, that he was failing Hinshaw. He sobbed with rage, at Hinshaw, at his own impotence. "I can't," he said to Hinshaw, who was pleading now with his eyes, desperate. "I can't!" he screamed.

And then he woke — screaming, sobbing. Trying to rise but held down by strong arms. Enveloping him as he wept and cried out, "I'm sorry! I'm sorry!" over and over until there was no breath in him, realizing eventually as he collapsed into himself that it was Lyric's arms, cradling him, holding him fast. He cried for a long time and she held on until he could cry no more and fell back into troubled sleep.

She was sitting on the edge of the bed, looking at him. He was naked, the sheets in a pile at the foot of the bed. Curled into a fetal position so tightly that every muscle and nerve and joint in his body ached with it. Faint light at the edge of the window shades. He closed his eyes again, lay there for awhile, hoping she would go away. But she didn't move. And he began to feel something vile and poisonous eating at the back of his mind. *Her. Here in my life. I don't need anybody and I don't need anybody needing me. I'm sick with needing. I'm sorry with needing.*

He opened his eyes. "What do want from me?"

He could see the hurt there, but to hell with it. She stared at him for a long time and then she got up off the bed. "Not a god-damn thing," she said. "I'll be out of here by tonight."

The panic hit him when he heard the front door slam shut. He vaulted out of the bed, rushed to the front of the house, tore the door open. She was fifty yards away on the sidewalk and he could see the anger in her ramrod back and pinched shoulders. "Wait!" he yelled. "I didn't mean it. Please!"

She kept walking. He started toward the sidewalk then felt a stab of pain in his foot. Sand spurs. And then he realized that he was here in his front yard without a stitch of clothing on. A kid on a tricycle on the other side of the street was pointing at him and giggling. He hobbled toward the house thinking, *I am naked all the way to my soul.*

* * * * *

He got dressed, thought about going to Poulos's, but decided that might not be the best thing to do just yet. *Leave her alone. Patch it up later.* So he went to work and spent the morning trying not to think about her. Or Hinshaw.

Late morning, he called Rayfield, the paint guy, and found out where Fred Wesley was working. On his lunch hour he showed up with a bag of Dairy Queen stuff. Fred Wesley was way up, standing in a bucket at the end of a crane contraption, painting the side of a tall brick smokestack at the site of what had once been Copernicus Manufacturing. You could still faintly see the letters of the old company name marching vertically down the side of the stack, but Fred Wesley was covering them with beige paint. Fred Wesley was alone, deftly maneuvering the bucket with a series of levers, intent on the work. Jonas watched him for a minute or so, then called up, "Hey, whatcha doing that for?"

Fred Wesley peered over the side of the bucket and broke out in a grin. "Cause it needs it."

"That makes sense."

"Yeah," Fred Wesley said, "I'm slow, but I ain't stupid." He flipped some levers and lowered the bucket, climbed out, and hugged Jonas. It felt good.

They ate in the shade of what had once been the loading dock of the plant. The whole place had gone to seed — windows broken, walls dingy with years of grime, paint flaking or gone altogether, weeds rampant. It was pretty depressing, Jonas thought, but then it suited his state of mind right now.

"What's going on here?" Jonas asked, waving at the smokestack.

"Daddy says they got some government money and they're gonna turn this place into an incinerator."

It took Jonas a moment. "You mean an incubator?"

"Yeah, that's it."

"New businesses."

"Uh-huh."

"That's a big job," Jonas said, nodding again at the smokestack.

"Coupla days. Daddy says it's a progress symbol. After I get done covering up the old stuff, I'm gonna paint the word 'Progress' on the stack. Big letters."

Progress, Jonas thought, was not a word he would ever have associated with Fleetwood Satterfield, or with Copernicus at large. Fleetwood had been mayor for as long as Jonas could remember, mayor of a town with a collective inferiority complex. Folks were satisfied just to have the potholes repaired and get electricity and water when they needed it, and as long as Fleetwood Satterfield could make

that happen, they were happy to keep re-electing him. But now —
progress?

"Gotta start somewhere," Jonas said, wondering what kind
of businesses might be attracted to a Copernicus incubator. He
thought about Lyric. A yoga studio? But then he remembered what
he had said to her.

Fred Wesley popped another French fry in his mouth and
chased it with a drag on his milkshake straw. "You don't look so hot,"
he said.

"I'm not so hot."

"You look like somebody that got drunk and ain't quite got
over it."

"Yeah, I kinda feel like shit."

They ate in silence for awhile, and even though he felt like
shit, the Dairy Queen stuff was going down okay and he thought the
afternoon might be better, at least until Lyric came back to the house.
If she came back. "How's it going with Christy Jo?" he asked.

Fred Wesley smiled. "Kiss and make up. And Maylene's
teaching her how to make stir fry. It's still a little iffy, but when she
gets good at it, you'll have to come back and try some."

"I'd be honored," Jonas said. "Fred Wesley, the other night
when the ruckus was going on at your place, your Daddy said something like 'I was afraid it would come to this.'"

"Yeah, Daddy didn't want me marrying Christy Jo."

"Why not?"

"He called her trailer trash."

"But you married her anyway."

"Me and Daddy had some words about that. But yeah, I just
went right ahead. We had a nice ceremony at the Church of Christ
and then we went on a honeymoon to Panama City. And you know,
Jonas, when I wake up in the middle of the night and I'm hugging
Christy Jo and feeling all warm and like I really belong someplace, I
think I did exactly the right thing. Sure, Christy Jo came from what
Mama calls the less-privileged side of town, and Maylene can be a
pain, but I used to think, 'Who's gonna marry a guy like me? I'm
slow, and I don't make a lot of money.' But most of the time, Christy
Jo thinks I'm okay."

"Fred Wesley," Jonas said, "I think you did exactly the right thing. I'm mighty happy for you. And Christy Jo."

"You ever think about getting married, Jonas?"

"Have never given it a thought. Besides, who would want to marry somebody like me? I'm missing two fingers, I walk with a limp, I don't have much of a job, and I'm a little messed up in the head."

"Well," Fred Wesley said, giving it some thought, "it would take just the right person."

"Yes it would."

"How about that girl that's living with you?"

"That's kinda shaky right now." Just saying it, he felt a lurch at the pit of his stomach, a sharp stab of pain in his shoulder, right about where the bullet went in. He put the rest of his burger aside.

Fred Wesley sucked noisily on the last of his milkshake, "Right after you went off to the Navy, I tried to join the National Guard," Fred Wesley said, "but they wouldn't take me. They said I couldn't pass the test."

"Why did you try to join the National Guard?"

"Well, you were off fighting, and you were my friend, and I thought I oughta do something."

It took a moment before Jonas could speak. "Well, all that's over too."

"Were you scared over there?" Fred Wesley asked.

"All the time."

"Was that the worst part? Being scared?"

Jonas thought about it. "Maybe it was. Even more than getting shot. Getting shot, that was a one-time deal. But being scared? That was an all-the-time deal."

"Doc Ainsley told me what you were doing over there. He said you were a kind of doctor."

"Kinda."

"Helping people."

"That was my job."

Fred Wesley broke into a grin. "You remember Cody Reighard and the cafeteria?"

"Sure."

"You busted his ass."

"More like his head."

"You was helping me, and that's when we started being friends."

Jonas felt tears, and he couldn't stop them. They leaked from his eyes and trickled down his cheeks. Fred Wesley didn't say a word, he just pulled a grimy piece of cloth out of a rear pocket and handed it to Jonas.

When he regained his composure he said, "I'm mighty glad you're my friend, Fred Wesley Satterfield." He stood up and Fred Wesley stood up and they had another good hug and then they both went back to work.

* * * * *

Just before five, he emptied the waste baskets and headed for the back alley and the dumpster. It was something he did every day, part of his routine, but when he opened the back door and started out, everything changed. *The narrow alley began to spin and shake until it collapsed into itself and became a street in a village and walls began to crumple into rubble and chaos let loose. Smoke, fire, explosions. Something punched him hard in the gut and then in the shoulder and the thigh and spun him around. He flattened himself against the side of the building, went to the ground, looking for escape. A door to his right and he crawled through it, away from the chaos, curled himself into a tight ball, freezing it all out. He could sense that the shadowy figures were there, watching him, moving closer. But then they left him there in his agony.*

It took a long time for the noise to go away and for him to realize that he was in the back hallway of the police station. He stifled a sob, and then he heard a voice in the back of his head. *I need...I need...*

He was waiting for her on the sidewalk outside Poulos's. Had been there all the time as dark came and the lights inside the café came on and he could see her moving around, absorbed in the work.

Now it was after nine and she was coming out. She saw him, turned abruptly away, but he grabbed her arm, spun her around. She slapped him. He took it. Then she went soft, something in her eyes. "Please," he said, "don't go."

"Why not?"

"Because I need you to stay."

"Why?"

"Because I'm scared and you're the only thing that makes any sense." He was crying again and making no effort to stop it. "Please," he said again, a whisper. "You don't have to sleep with me. I'll take the couch. Just stay."

"And what about you, Jonas? Are you gonna stay?"

"I've got to. I've got stuff to take care of."

He let go of her arm and stifled his crying. The sidewalk was empty, customers all gone. But then Poulos showed up at the front door to lock up, saw them there, opened the door. "Are you guys okay?"

"Yeah," she said. "It's okay, Poulos."

"See you tomorrow."

"Yeah."

Poulos shut the door and Jonas heard the key in the lock and just stood there, staring at his feet. Then he felt her hand on his cheek.

"I don't want anything from you," she said. There was a long silence, and then she said, "That's not right."

He looked up into her eyes. Softness there. It didn't show up much, but it was there now.

"Jonas," she said, "you are the most gentle person I've ever met. And I've known some gold-plated assholes, so I know the difference. I've been trying real hard not to like you too much, but God help me, I'm afraid I do. Way too much. It doesn't make any goddamn sense, Jonas, because I'm not gonna be here a whole lot longer and after I'm gone I might not ever see you again. But for now..."

"Then..."

She shrugged, then she took his hand and they started toward home.

TWELVE

He told Carl about Hinshaw, about the alley behind the police station, the figures that kept showing up, drawing closer. It took him a good while until he haltingly got it all out, and then he slumped in his chair, utterly drained.

Carl gave him a minute to compose himself. "And how are you handling it?"

"I'm scared shitless. And I feel old."

"You've lived a lifetime," Carl said. "Now you're living another one."

"Will I ever get past it?"

"Not completely. It's part of you. But what we want is for you to come to look at it as memory — bad memory for sure — but just memory. And put it in its place so you can move on."

"I don't want to end up like Ray Willis."

"He couldn't get past it."

"No."

They were silent for a moment while Carl scribbled. He looked up. "You know that you're not alone in this. I see others who come back with bad — really bad — stuff to deal with. Some deal with it, some don't."

"Like Ray."

"It's a different kind of war."

"In what way?"

"It's something I call the Shitty Surprise Syndrome."

"And?"

"Bad shit coming from out of nowhere."

"You got that right."

"The world wars, everybody on all sides knew who the enemy was. We're over here, they're over there. We wear uniforms, they wear uniforms. They attack, we attack. Kill each other. But we know who we're killing and who's killing us. This now, it's not like that. Can't tell the good guys from the bad guys. Shit blowing up in our faces. IED's, RPG's, some woman in a burka with dynamite strapped to her chest. So how do you deal with that?"

"You keep your guard up or get your ass blown off. Or maybe you get your ass blown off anyway."

"Right. It blows up in your face. And when it's over, and you come home, you're still keeping your guard up. Watching everything and everybody. Avoiding crowds. Hyper vigilance."

"Mom is trying to get me to go to church with her, but the idea of all those people...I can't handle it."

"Go into a room with a bunch of people, you've got your back to the wall, keeping everything in front of you. Hard to do that in church."

"Will I ever get over that?"

Carl shrugged, "You can come to terms with it."

Jonas shook his head. "I don't know how."

Carl leaned forward in his chair.

"Jonas, we've talked about you as a caregiver. How you're compelled to help people. The kid at the golf place. The down-on-her-luck young woman who's living with you. It's your most basic instinct. But it has its perils. When you open yourself up to other people, you pull back the curtain on places and people and situations that you've been trying so hard to keep locked away."

"So am I supposed to stop helping people?"

Carl smiled. "As if you could."

"So what?"

"You either come to grips with the locked-away stuff...or you find a corner to hide in for the rest of your life and try to become who you're not. I think you're in hand-to-hand combat with that right now. Incredibly hard choice, but it's kind of shit or get off the pot."

Jonas stared at him, heat rising at the back of his neck. "Fuck you, Carl."

Carl sat back. "Let's go back to the guy you were talking about. Hinshaw?"

"Yeah."

"Do you think your memory of that was accurate?"

"It was like it was happening right then and there."

"And what were you thinking when you saw him."

Jonas froze. Tried to speak, nothing. A punch in the gut, bile in his throat. Then a great rush of sadness. "I said...I kept saying...I'm sorry. I'm sorry."

"Sorry he was wounded?"

Jonas started to cry. "I couldn't help him. I think he knew that. So fucked up he wasn't gonna make it. Just wanted somebody... me...to be there with him while he died. But I couldn't."

"Why not?"

He struggled, trying to put a word on it. Finally, "Because...I failed."

"You had to move on, right?"

"I guess."

"And you saved some others."

"That's what...they say."

And that was the end of it. He couldn't go on with it any more right now, couldn't take the next step beyond Hinshaw, whose eyes — terrified but resigned — still bore into him everywhere he looked. His eyes were clenched shut, but Hinshaw was still there.

Carl gave him a long time to ease back from it before he said, "From what I've been able to learn about what happened, there are a lot of Hinshaws out there."

Jonas nodded.

"You can't keep them locked away, no matter how hard you try. You can try to insulate yourself from it with stuff like drugs and booze, but they're a dead-end street. And at the end of the street, the light goes out." He paused, giving Jonas time to feel desperation welling up at his deepest part. "You don't have to do this by yourself. You've got friends, the people you've told me about. If absolutely necessary, the VA can admit you to the hospital. Short of that, we can try things like hypnosis, psychedelics, some other new stuff that's being worked on."

"I am not going to be in a fucking hospital," Jonas said hotly. "I'd rather die in a gutter than be in another hospital."

"Okay." A long moment, then, "There's another thing you should consider. Writing it down."

"I'm not much of a writer," Jonas said. "And how can I write when I don't remember, and don't want to?"

"You do remember. Things are coming back to you. Start with those. Write as much as you can about Hinshaw and the figures and the alley blowing up, things that have come to you in bits and pieces. Write about those, and the chances are the rest will follow. Don't worry about whether it's good writing or not, just be honest. Jonas Boulware has a story. Tell it."

Jonas stood to go. Time up. And then he remembered. "Something I've been meaning to ask you. You said you grew up in Copernicus. Was your family affected when the plant shut down?"

Carl thought about it for a moment. "My father was the plant superintendent. My mother worked in customer service. Good jobs one day, no jobs the next."

"What did they do? What did *you* do?"

"I was the oldest of four. In college. So was my younger sister. I dropped out for a year and worked so she could stay in school. My parents moved away, found other work. Not as good, but something to get by."

"You were probably pretty pissed at my family," Jonas said.

Carl nodded. "Sure was for awhile. But I just got over it." He waited for a moment then said, "You either do or you don't. If you don't, you wither away from the inside out. And that's what I'm saying to you, Jonas. Do."

* * * * *

"**I** want you to go over to Baptist and read a story to some children," Gladys said over the phone.

"When?"

"On your lunch hour."

"I can't."

"You can't or you won't?"

"Okay, I won't."

"Jonas, you need to get over yourself."

He felt weariness come over him. "Mom, I'm trying. I really am. But it's not easy for me right now. So the thought of a crowd of squirming Baptist kids…"

"There's Methodist and Presbyterian too."

"…and probably a few heathens thrown in. No Mom, I won't do it."

"Then I'll have to do it and you'll have to come sit with Rodney."

"That, I can do."

It had been a couple of days since he saw Rodney, and Jonas thought he had declined a lot — color terrible, even more slackness in his look, spending most of his time in bed. Gladys had her purse in her hand. "If he needs something, he'll tell you. The home health care people will be here at one, so you can leave then. I'm baking cookies at the Senior Center this afternoon."

"I didn't know there was a Senior Center."

"At the Presbyterian."

"And you're helping out."

"Of course."

Jonas walked to the door with her. "He doesn't look good."

"I think he looks just fine, Jonas. But you're the medical expert." There was a real edge in it. Was she that pissed with him for avoiding the little Baptists? But he let it go. "He's making a lot of progress. He's writing now."

"What?"

"I got him a scratch pad and a pencil and he can write things down, like when he needs a drink of water. It's not the whole words, but you can make it out if you try. So try. Encourage him."

Rodney appeared to be asleep. Jonas sat in the room with him, looking out the window, across the sweep of the golf course to the clubhouse up on the rise. He thought about Ben, about Lieutenant, about all Carl had said, about what it might take to pick up that golf club again.

Rodney made a low, guttural sound. Eyes open, looking at Jonas.

"Hi Dad."

Rodney motioned with a jerk of his head toward the bedside table, and Rodney realized he wanted the pad and pencil. He handed the pad to him and Rodney held up his left hand. Jonas helped him wedge the pencil clawlike in the hand and then he painfully scrawled

BTH

It took Jonas a moment. "You want to go to the bathroom?"
Rodney nodded.

Jonas pulled back the sheet and blanket, trying not to stare. Everything below Rodney's head seemed wasted, shriveled in on itself, more so than the last time he was here, a week ago. He was pretty easy to lift and carry to the bathroom. Jonas got him settled and then waited outside in the hall, the door open just a crack. It took a long time, but then he heard Rodney make the sound and he went in and cleaned him up and started back to the bedroom with him. He stopped. "I think you need some fresh air." So he carried Rodney to the living room and eased him into the wheelchair, went back to the bedroom and got the blanket, tucked it around Rodney, and headed outside — down the ramp, around the corner of the house to the patio. He parked Rodney so he could see the country club and pulled up a chair. They sat there for a while, Jonas holding the pad and pencil in case Rodney needed to ask for something. Then Jonas said, "It's good. You can write."

Grunt.

"A guy told me I should write stuff down. Stuff about the war. I don't know if I can do it."

They sat for a long time in silence. Rodney's head drooped and rested on his chest.

"Then there's golf," Jonas said softly so that he didn't wake Rodney. "I picked up a club out at Lieutenant's place and made a swing with it. Helping this kid named Ben who seems to need somebody just to put a little effort into him. May not come to anything, but anyway...I picked up the club and swung it and it wasn't all bad. And then I thought about how it ended back there at the state tournament. And I thought, 'Am I gonna let him keep that away from me?' And then I thought, 'Maybe not.'"

More silence and then Rodney raised his head, looked at Jonas, blinked, motioned for the pad and pencil. The stubby pencil hovered for a half-minute over the paper and then

SORY

Jonas stared for a long time. "Me too, Dad. I'm sorry about all of it. It just never worked out back there, did it. And now," he held up his left hand, "I'm all shot to pieces, here and," tapping his head, "here. I'm sorry about that, too. And I'm really sorry about what's happened to you, Dad." He stopped because he couldn't go on for a while and then he said, "So you're sorry and I'm sorry. And I guess we'll just have to leave it at that. Except, I'm not pissed any more, at least not at you. I just don't have it in me. So take that with you, wherever you're headed."

* * * * *

Lieutenant's after work, surprised to find Ben there. He was standing behind one of the mats, staring at his golf bag, shoulders slumped, unmoving.

"Ben..."

"Go away and leave me alone."

"Ben, I want to apologize...busting in like I did the other day at your place. I think I scared you. I'm sorry I did."

"And are you sorry you sent the cop guy and the social worker out there?"

"I was worried about you. But they said everything was okay."

"You shouldn'ta done it."

"Like I said, I was worried. This guy Oscar..."

"He's gone."

"I'm glad. Are you?"

"Yeah."

"He didn't seem like the kind of guy you'd want around."

Ben was silent, his eyes searching Jonas.

"Is your Mom okay?"

Ben shrugged.

"Look, if there's anything I can do..."

"Just stay away, okay. Just stay the fuck away."

"All right. Look, Ben, I know that what we've been doing here, it's all about golf. But I've come to think of you as a friend."

Ben shook his head fiercely. "I don't have any friends and I don't need any friends."

"Okay. But if you ever need anything, if you're having a tough time, come to me."

"Just stick to the golf, okay?"

Jonas took a nine-iron out of Ben's bag. The stamp, embedded in the metal: **BL**. "You said you just found these."

"Yeah. They may have been my Dad's."

"Do you know anything about him? Name? Where he is?"

"No. Mom doesn't talk about it." A long pause. Jonas waited. "I used to think he might come back some day and make everything okay. But I gave up on that."

"Okay. Let's hit some golf balls."

"You first."

Jonas placed a ball on the mat, took a stance, feeling the club strange and unfamiliar in his hands. His grip, all messed up with the two fingers missing. *Have to compensate, a little more pressure with the right hand.* He thought about Rodney. *Do I really mean it, that I'm not pissed any more? Let's see.* He swung, made decent contact, sent the ball a hundred yards or so downrange. *Not much for a nine-iron. Used to hit a nine 145. But up and straight. And no, I'm not pissed.* He looked back at Ben, who was standing there with his arms crossed, all closed in on himself. "Your turn."

They worked for a half-hour with the nine iron and Ben seemed to settle into it. Good shoulder turn, control the back swing, hips first, then swing through. Ben was hitting them out there about 130. Lieutenant came out and watched for a while, wordless, then went back to the pro shop.

When they were finished, Jonas said, "I don't guess you want me to take you home."

"Got my bike."

"Okay."

"Did good today."

"Maybe."

"Again tomorrow?"

"Maybe."

"Remember what I said, Ben. If you need..."

"I won't," Ben cut him off. "I'm sure of that."

Lieutenant was unpacking a new set of irons. "Doc's," he said. "He thinks a new set of irons will take ten strokes off his score. I keep telling him, it ain't the arrow, it's the Indian."

"Want me to take 'em to him?"

"Yeah. You do that. And tell him what I said about the arrow and the Indian."

"Well, he already knows you're full of shit, Lieutenant."

Lieutenant grinned. "As he keeps telling me."

Jonas watched while Lieutenant finished unpacking, removed the protective cellophane from the irons, and put them back in the box. "I watched you with the kid today," Lieutenant said. "You're a natural teacher."

"Just trying to help."

"That's what you do, Jonas. Try to help. You're really patient with him."

"I think he needs it. It's pretty rough out there where he lives. One thing, though, he told me the guy who was living there, Oscar, is gone. I could tell Ben was scared of him."

"You know, Jonas, you could get your PGA professional card and be an instructor somewhere."

"I never thought about that." He held up his left hand. "You think I could be an instructor with this?"

"You hit a golf ball, didn't you?"

"It didn't go very far."

"I could work with you, see what you can do to compensate. But you don't need that to be a teacher. You know a good swing when you see it. The one you had back yonder was one of the prettiest I've ever seen."

"I'll think about it," Jonas said.

"While you're sitting down there at Kayo's place, answering the telephone and talking with Milo on the radio."

"It's a job, Lieutenant."

"People bug you much? Dropping by?"

"Some did for a while. Find an excuse to go see what's left of Jonas Boulware. There was this one girl I was in school with. Came in, sat down, spent a half hour telling me all about herself. When she got up to leave, she said, 'Did you kill anybody over there?' I wanted to say, 'No, dickhead, I tried to save people.' But I didn't say that. I just said, 'No, never saw a need to.'"

"Did you save some?"

"Yes. Lost a couple, too."

"But you tried."

"That was my job."

Lieutenant wrapped some tape around the box of Doc's new irons and handed them over. "Come out here and save some poor dickhead from a bad slice."

"If I get worn out with answering the telephone and talking to Milo on the radio, I'll consider your offer."

* * * * *

To Doc's with the golf clubs. It was moving on toward evening and Doc was in his usual place by the backyard koi pond with a drink at his elbow and a book in hand. "Have a seat," he said, "while I finish this chapter."

Jonas laid the box of clubs at Doc's feet and waited, watching the koi flitting and swirling about. Just watching, not thinking, letting the fish take over his mind. Doc finally put the book aside, rose, opened the box and stood there admiring the clubs for a moment. "These will take ten strokes off my score," he said.

"Yeah, that's what Lieutenant said. He also said something about arrows and Indians."

Doc snorted. "Lieutenant is full of shit."

"I tell him that all the time."

Doc picked up a club, stepped to the side, and took a few swings, making little divots in the grass.

"Lieutenant said I should be an instructor."

Doc kept swinging. "And?"

"I told him I'd think about it."

Doc put the club aside and sat back down. "How's it going with Carl?"

"Okay."

"Just okay?"

"Doc, it's beginning to come back. Bits and pieces." He told Doc about Hinshaw, about the alley behind the police station. "I don't know if I'll ever put it all together, and I'd like to keep it down where it's been, but I don't guess I have any choice about it."

"How are you handling it?"

"Not well."

"Is Carl helping?"

"Yeah. I feel comfortable with him. He says I can't take care of the world unless I take care of myself."

"Caring about other people is at the absolute core of who you are, Jonas. And I'm guessing it's at war with reality. What you're really looking for is coming to some sort of peace with that."

"Carl told me about what happened with his family, with him, when the plant closed."

"And what did he say about that?"

"He said he just got over it."

"He's a good man, a fine human being," Doc said. "Stick with him."

Jonas stood up. "Better go. Lyric'll be home before long."

"How's that going?"

"All right."

"Is she your girlfriend?"

"I don't know what she is, Doc. But she's there, at least for now, and I guess that's pretty good. I like her a lot."

"There's all kinds of therapy, Jonas."

"Probably. I told Carl, I feel old. Ancient. I even talk like an old man sometimes. But she reminds me that I'm not so old after all. Is that therapy? If so, I'm gonna go home and try it."

* * * * *

*He was on a street in a village. There were the piles of rubble, shells of buildings, stench of death and rot, a burned out car. But no Marines. It was just him, and he was looking frantically for the others, for the presence of other human beings so he wouldn't feel so alone here in the aching emptiness of the street with the smells and the fear clutching at him. Then suddenly the RPG's started coming, one after another, screaming down the empty street, exploding all around him, cratering the ground, making the rubble dance. **WHUMP! WHUMP! WHUMP!***

And then he was bolt upright in bed, eyes wide, and she was beside him, her hand clutching his arm. "What!" he screamed.

"It's the door! Jonas, there's somebody at the door."

He staggered out of bed, into the living room. She was right behind him. He reached for the doorknob, opened it, stared into the dark. And then he saw. Ben. Wearing nothing but a pair of baggy shorts. Crying, screaming, covered with blood. "I killed the mother-fucker! I killed him!"

He called Kayo, left Ben with Lyric, met Kayo at the trailer. Oscar was on the floor — skull caved in, face looking like it had been through a meat grinder. Blood everywhere. A nine-iron nearby, the head covered with bits of flesh and hair. Oscar was naked from the waist down.

Jonas staggered outside and threw up, sat heaving with grief in the weeds. Not for Oscar. He didn't give a fuck about Oscar. Kayo came out after a minute, sat near Jonas on the stoop. He said, "Misty's back yonder in the bedroom. Passed out, looks like she was beat up pretty bad."

An ambulance came for Misty, and then the crime scene crew from the sheriff's department showed up, taking photos and samples, measuring stuff. Kayo said, "I'm gonna have to take him in."

"Can't he just stay with me for awhile?"

"He's killed somebody, Jonas."

"All right. Give me thirty minutes. I just want to make sure he's all right."

"Twenty minutes. And don't ask him any questions."

Lyric had him cleaned up, wearing a pair of Jonas's shorts and a tee shirt. He looked petrified, sitting on the sofa in the living room. He couldn't keep his hands still. They knotted and unknotted, fluttered around his head, plucked at the hem of the shorts. Lyric looked spooked, too — wide-eyed and ashen.

Jonas sat next to him, afraid to touch for fear of what it might set off. He looked at his watch. Ten minutes. "Your Mom's okay," Jonas said.

"He beat the shit out her."

"She's going to the hospital. They'll take care of her."

"And where am I going?"

"Kayo's gonna take care of you. He's a good man."

They sat in silence for a minute and then it all came pouring out. "Oscar came back. He had a bunch of money, a drug deal. He and Mama were back there in the bedroom snorting some junk and then they started arguing and it got really loud and then I could hear him hitting her. I banged on the door and he came running out. And then he threw me down and tried to fuck me in the ass. I got away and got the club and started hitting him and I couldn't stop." He collapsed against the back of the sofa and his hands were quiet and so was the rest of him.

Kayo was there in a couple of minutes and Jonas walked with them to Kayo's car. Kayo put Ben in the back seat and closed the door.

"He told me what happened," Jonas said.

"I told you not to ask him any questions."

"I didn't. Not a thing. He just opened up on his own and spilled his guts."

"What did he say?"

Jonas told him. Then, "What are you gonna do with him?"

"Take him to the jail." When Jonas started to protest, Kayo held up his hand. "They've got a place for juveniles. He'll be safe."

"Are you gonna charge him?"

"Of course."

"Can I see him?"

"No, you can't. This is an investigation, Jonas. You've gotta stay out of it. If you don't, I'll have to arrest you too."

It was not quite light when he woke Doc up, told him every-thing. Doc listened without interrupting. When Jonas was finished, Doc said, "I'm sorry, Jonas. I know you've tried to help the boy. But it's out of your hands now."

"Maybe not."

"Don't go getting yourself in trouble."

"Thanks for the advice, Doc. But I really just need one thing from you. I need to know who Ben's father is."

Doc ruminated on it for a bit and then nodded and said, "Byrd."

THIRTEEN

Byrd. Step-brother he barely knew any more, or ever had, for that matter. Son of Gordon Laycock the Embezzler, already twelve years old when Jonas was born. Byrd resented the hell out of Jonas and let him know it from the beginning. He was fiercely possessive of everything he had, marked it all with his initials: ***B.L.*** Jonas — both intrigued and terrified — kept his distance. And that's the way it was.

Byrd was a spectacularly gifted athlete, superb at everything — football, basketball, baseball, track and field, golf. When he was thirteen he won the Copernicus Country Club Men's Championship. When he was fifteen he made All-State in both football and basketball. When he was sixteen he pitched Copernicus High School to the state championship in baseball. And Rodney was all over it.

So were a lot of college coaches. Before Byrd's senior year even began, he had offers, in every sport, and they kept coming. Rodney was all over that, too. He established himself as arbiter, filter and chief advisor. On first name basis with every coach in every sport who salivated over Byrd. There was a steady stream of them in the house — earnest, big-shouldered men from schools large and small who sat in the living room and made their pitches, usually just to Rodney and Byrd. Gladys busied herself in the kitchen, brought coffee and pound cake, and then went back to the kitchen. Jonas thought it was all pretty boring.

In the end, Byrd went to Auburn because Auburn promised him he could play both football and baseball. He and Rodney argued about that. Byrd, as good an arm as he had, wasn't all that interested in baseball. But Rodney, the old major leaguer, kept hammering at him about it. "One play, one bad injury, and football is toast," Rodney kept saying. "Baseball? Hell, Byrd, you got a million dollar arm and it can take you all the way to the top." It seemed to

Jonas, watching and listening from a distance, that Rodney finally just wore him down.

Byrd had been a quarterback in high school — he was cocky, he liked to run things, and he had a rifle for an arm — but Auburn already had a good quarterback, so they moved him to wide receiver. In his sophomore year he was All-SEC, and by the time he was a senior there was talk of a high pick in the NFL draft.

Rodney was all in. The house was awash in orange and blue and they went to all the games. The first few times it was exciting to Jonas — the crowds, the noise, the combat on the field — but by the end of the first season he was desperately sick of the trips, long and short, and Rodney's can't-shut-up running commentary on everything Byrd. He sat quietly in the back seat of the car for endless miles, and for interminable fidgeting hours on hard-on-your-ass stadium seats, and wished to God it would all soon end and Byrd would go to the New York Giants and Rodney would go to hell.

It ended in the third quarter against Mississippi State on a drizzly October afternoon in Starkville. Jonas wasn't paying attention — Auburn was leading and he was physically miserable from the rain dripping down the back of his neck — so it wasn't until later when he saw the video that he knew how it happened. For a few seconds, Byrd was open in the corner of the end zone, but the ball was late getting there. Byrd and two defensive backs went up for it and then ended up in a sprawl of bodies. He didn't see it, but he heard the snap, so loud that it cut through everything. The pile down in the end zone untangled, except for Byrd, who lay there writhing on the turf, clutching at his left leg. It seemed that every soul in the stadium rose as one, dead silent. Jonas looked at the end zone, then up at Gladys standing next to him, saw the utter shock and terror on her face, and knew that something terrible had happened to Byrd.

The leg was shattered just above the ankle. There were operations — steel rods and plates and screws — and long months of therapy. Rodney and Gladys adopted an attitude of frantic optimism. One or the other — often both — were constantly at Byrd's side.

Jonas, through it all, was simply an afterthought. Concern for Byrd morphed into resentment, then a kind of smoldering rage that he kept to himself. He was nine years old, and he began to think of himself as an orphan. He spent weekends with Doc Ainsley while Rodney and Gladys were with Byrd. He could tell Rodney didn't like that, but he liked even less taking Jonas with them. "All he does is mope around and whine," Rodney said. That wasn't true, Jonas thought. He moped, but he kept his damned mouth shut. It was a lot better with Doc, who had lost Evelyn and seemed to genuinely welcome Jonas's company.

Finally, the surgeons told Byrd and Rodney and Gladys that it was all over. They had pieced Byrd together as best they could, but he would always walk with a limp and he would never play again. Not football, of course, but also not baseball. A right-handed pitcher who couldn't push off on his left leg was no pitcher at all.

Byrd came home. He had no interest in finishing his degree at Auburn. He had no interest in much of anything. He was pissed off at the world. Gladys dogged his every step — solicitous, mournful — until Byrd yelled at her to leave him alone. Rodney and Byrd avoided each other. Rodney was pissed too, and Jonas — even at nine — was smart enough to figure that it had something to do with Rodney's own athletic disaster, his great disappointment. Rodney's one attempt at connecting with Byrd was to ask him to play golf. When they got home at the end of the day, the mutual rage was so thick it made Jonas cringe. After that, Byrd disappeared for days at a time. And after a month of that, he disappeared altogether. Jonas had not heard a word about him — from Gladys or anyone else — for years.

Until now. Now, here was Doc telling him that Byrd had spent much of that first month's disappearance shacked up with a young woman named Misty Cameron, a former high school classmate. When he left for good, he left evidence that his sperm was just fine. Misty Cameron had come looking for Byrd, who was by now gone. Misty was two months gone herself. Seven months later, she gave birth.

Of course, Jonas thought. There was that familiar look about the kid. The old set of golf clubs stamped with **B.L.** But most of all there was just the fact of Byrd the asshole. Like a long hand reaching from the grave.

"He's your nephew," Doc said.

"Does Byrd know?"

"I don't know." Doc waited for a moment, pulling at his nose, before he said, "You'll have to ask your mother about that. I do know she bought a trailer for Misty, and she's been sending money every month."

"I'm not surprised," Jonas said. "I'd be surprised if she hadn't."

He went to see Gladys. "Does Byrd know he has a son?"

"No."

"Why not?"

Gladys pursed her lips and looked distant. "We just couldn't afford any more scandal."

"My God. So you just paid off the woman…Ben's mother… and kept it all quiet."

"Yes."

"Does Rodney know?"

"Of course not. I've got my own money. Papa left money for me, and Gordon and Rodney never got their hands on it."

"Do you ever see Ben?"

"The child? No, I never have."

"You just send money."

"Yes."

"You know he's in jail."

"I heard that."

"Where is Byrd?"

That stopped her cold. She shook her head.

"Do you see him, hear from him?"

"I don't," she said, "have anything to say about that."

But there was Kayo, and all the information at a lawman's disposal, and there was Google. It was easy to track down Byrd Laycock, or at least who and where he was. He was a high school football coach in Oregon, a fairly successful one, with a wife and two kids, both girls. So Jonas knew, and now he had to figure out what to do with the knowing.

Kayo told him that Ben had been charged with manslaughter, that Fleetwood Satterfield had been appointed as his attorney, that the District Attorney was looking through the case. It might qualify as self defense, especially considering Ben's age. Or might not. "There's one other thing Ben told the Sheriff. That scumbag Oscar made him play with himself."

"Jerk off," Jonas said.

"Yeah. While the guy watched. Said he'd beat up Ben's mother if he didn't, or if he told."

Jonas felt sick. "I wish I coulda been the one with that golf club."

"No you don't."

"I didn't do enough."

"You did all you could. Now stop beating yourself about the head and shoulders with it."

He went to see Ramona, the social worker who had gone to the trailer with Kayo. "I can't tell you anything about an ongoing case," she said.

"Okay, hypothetical. Would I qualify as a foster parent?"

Ramona gave him a long look. "Jonas, I'm afraid not. It's your age, and Kayo says you're in psychological treatment, and you have a live-in girlfriend. Social Services would never approve that. Here's another hypothetical. If a juvenile came from a home where he...or she...were in danger, we would of course step in. If that juvenile were charged with a serious crime, and for some reason the charges were dropped...well, the child could not go back to a dangerous situation. Foster care, and we have some qualified, loving people we can turn to. Over time, our goal is always to re-unite families. But our over-riding concern is for the health, welfare and safety of the child." She waited for awhile, letting him absorb it. "Does that help?"

"Some."

"You understand, we're dealing in hypotheticals here."

"Yes ."

"So that's all I can say."

He went to Kayo and told him what he planned to do, and then he went home and told Lyric. "You do what you have to," she said.

"It's what I have to."

"Jonas, I gotta tell you, I've almost got enough money for a car."

He pleaded. "Don't go until I get this taken care of."

"Okay. But don't be long at it."

So he got on the phone and bought an airline ticket to Oregon.

* * * * *

The high school was nestled in a valley guarded by mountains and tall timber, at the edge of a little crossroads community. The football field was out back, and there was a scraggle of kids out there in shorts. And a coach.

He found the gate. Closed, but not padlocked, so he pushed it open and passed the concession stand and the bleachers and stopped at the edge of the field. It was in pristine shape — a thick, manicured stand of grass, yardage lines marked neatly — a contrast to the rest of the school. He stood there for a moment and watched until some of the kids pointed in his direction and the coach turned and yelled, "Hey, this is a closed practice." Jonas didn't move. "You can't come in here." He started toward Jonas. "You'll have to leave," he called out. "No visitors, no exceptions."

Byrd had gone a bit to seed. There was a paunch ballooning the bottom of his tee shirt, deep lines around his mouth and eyes, a stubble of beard. He was trotting by the time he reached Jonas, looking pissed. "You deaf or something?" When he reached for Jonas's arm, Jonas said, "Hello, Byrd. Been a long time."

"My little brother," he introduced Jonas to the kids. There weren't many of them, but they were sturdy like lumberjacks and looked to be in great shape. He stood on the sidelines and watched while they ran drills and Byrd was everywhere — fussing, encouraging, teaching. He seemed very good at it, and the kids paid attention and responded. It was spirited.

There was a convenience store carved out of the woods at the crossroads and they got sandwiches and sodas and ate at a picnic table out to the side next to a creek that splashed and burbled. Everything was green and tall and seemed to press in on you. Jonas didn't know if he could live in a place like this, certainly not now when there was so much else pressing in.

Why Oregon? And how? One of Byrd's coaches at Auburn had taken a job at Oregon State after Byrd's last season, after the catastrophe. Byrd moved out, lived with the coach and his wife, finished school, took a job as a graduate assistant with the football team. That lasted for a couple of years. "I had a drinking problem," Byrd said matter-of-factly. He was asked to leave, and then this little high school took a chance on him and he had been here ever since. A wife who had grown up here, a couple of daughters. "Amanda saved my life," he said. "I was a mess. Haven't had a drink in ten years. You've heard country songs about a woman getting a man turned around? Well, she turned me around."

Byrd rambled on for awhile about his life, the football team. They had won a state championship a couple of years back, might again. Finally he asked, "And what about you? What you been up to?"

"Hasn't Mom told you?"

"I haven't talked to Mom in, I don't know, three years."

"I joined the Navy," Jonas said. "I'm out now. Back in Copernicus, working for Kayo Grissett at the police station." And that was it. Byrd didn't ask for details and that was fine. Nothing he wanted to share with Byrd Laycock. Byrd was a stranger, always had been.

They finished their sandwiches and there was an awkward moment when neither seemed to know what was next. Then Byrd said, "Jonas, why did you come out here?"

"To see about your son."

"I don't have a son."

"Mom and Doc Ainsley say you do. With Misty Cameron."

He went deathly pale. And then he said, quite softly, "Fuck."

"His name is Ben. He'll be fourteen in a couple of weeks. He's in some trouble."

"I don't have a son," Byrd repeated, and Jonas could see the old, belligerent, pissed-off Byrd surfacing. And no asking for details.

"Mom's been sending Misty some money every month since Ben was born. Bought a house trailer for 'em."

"Then why hasn't Mom said something to me?"

"You'd have to ask her," Jonas said.

They sat there in silence for a while, and Jonas could see the wheels turning. "I can't do anything about it," Byrd said finally. "It would wreck everything. Mandy, the girls…"

Jonas nodded. "Okay. I just wanted to you to know."

"Have you told the kid?"

"Ben. No, I haven't told Ben about you, haven't told him that I'm his uncle. And there's no way anybody can prove any of it without a DNA test. And I guess you're not gonna go there."

"Hell, no."

He stood. "I'll tell you this, I'm gonna do everything I can to make sure *you* never hear another word about this. From anybody. You don't have to worry, Byrd. Just take care of yourself. Live a long and happy life."

* * * * *

He went to Doc.

"You tried," Doc said. "You tried more than I can imagine anybody doing to help a kid you don't really know that well."

"Well enough."

"I suspect he reminds you of you. His situation is way tougher than yours, but there's just enough that's familiar."

"I don't know what to do, Doc. He'll either go to juvenile detention if the charge sticks, or to foster care if it doesn't. And eventually he'll end up back in that miserable shithole of a trailer with that miserable slut junkie of a mother."

Doc said softly, "Let it go, Jonas, at least for now. Maybe down the road you can do something to help Ben, but for now, you've done all any human could do."

"I failed him, Doc. Just like I failed all those guys I was supposed to take care of over there."

Doc sighed. "I think you need to go talk to Carl about that."

* * * * *

But before that there was Gladys. He told her about Byrd and Oregon. "It wouldn't do for Byrd to come back here," she said, "for anything."

"Why not?"

"It would just remind everybody of the scandal."

"And that's what matters more to you than anything in the world."

"Our family destroyed this town."

"And you've spent your life trying to make amends."

"Yes I have!"

He sat there for a long time, not speaking, thinking about what a sad life she had led with the sword hanging over her head. Maybe that was why she never crossed Rodney. Afraid people might talk. That was wretched.

"There's just one thing. You've got to keep sending the money."

"But…"

"If you don't, I'll tell."

He stood to go. "You've let one thieving asshole ruin your life. Terrified of scandal, of what people might think. Held hostage by the whole goddamn town, at least in your own mind. I don't know why you wouldn't ever take up for me with Dad, but maybe it has something to do with all that. I don't know. But I'll tell you what I do know, Mom. I really and truly feel sorry for you. It's a miserable way to live."

FOURTEEN

There was a Ford Explorer at the curb when he got home. A few dings and scratches, paint fading on top, but other than that it looked pretty solid. "I bought it from Poulos," she said.

They sat on the front steps.

He was numb. Couldn't feel a single part of his body. "So you've got the car."

"Another thing. A guy came in last Thursday when I was singing, and after, he said he was a record producer and I needed to get my butt to Nashville and see if I can make it."

It took a great deal of effort for him to ask, "When are you going?"

"Tomorrow."

He could feel himself collapsing in on himself, the way Gladys had. He couldn't speak. Couldn't even nod. She took his hand. His own felt like ice, desperate for warmth. "I've been upfront from the get-go." His eyes were on the ground, but he could feel her looking at him. "You could come with me," she said.

He looked up finally, summoned breath. "No. You don't need a basket case hanging around while you see if you can make it."

"Maybe later?"

He shrugged.

They made love in the evening. He woke just before dawn, pulled on shorts and a tee shirt, left her sleeping while he went for a long walk — through town, out to the country club and the cart paths, back past Glady's house (he had long ago ceased to think of it as home) and Doc's, then back to the bungalow.

She was up, dressed, packed, waiting for him. He kissed her and held on as long as he could, then let her go. "Good luck. You're gonna be terrific."

"So are you," she said. "Don't forget me."

"Couldn't if I tried."

"And what I said about later…"

And then she was gone.

* * * * *

He went to work. Kayo had sweet-talked Tilda into coming back and handling the radio and phone while he was gone to Oregon, but Kayo said she had grumbled about it the whole time, and he was happy to see her go.

Jonas hoped the work would take his mind off all the other, at least for a little while, but his brain was everywhere but the police station, full of chaos coming at him from all sides — Gladys, Rodney, Doc, Lyric, Ben, the platoon. Circuits completely overloaded, what might be the real world locked away, interrupted every once in awhile by a ringing phone or squawking radio.

At mid-afternoon, lost in thought, he looked up to see a tall, rawboned man in a black suit standing there, leaning across with his hands flat on Jonas's desk. "Can I help you?"

"Jonas, we want you to come witness to our congregation."

"What?"

"I'm the pastor at Pentecostal Holiness and we want you to come Wednesday night to Bible study and witness."

"Witness what?"

"How the Lord laid his hands on you and brought you through the fire."

"You're kidding."

The pastor looked surprised. "What do you mean?"

"I mean you must be kidding."

"But the Lord…"

"And what about those guys who didn't make it, who got their heads blown off and their guts torn out. Did the Lord have his hands on them too? If so, he messed up big time."

The pastor raised himself up. He was really tall and his face was really red. "Young man…"

"Look, preacher, if I'da been God, I'da said. 'Don't go to Afghanistan. If you do, you're on your own. I ain't going because I'm liable to get my ass shot off.'"

"You little heathen shit!"

He marched out and Jonas had to sit there for a good while, ignoring the phone and the radio, while he came back to earth. It made him sick, and he finally got up and went to the bathroom and threw up.

He was back at his desk, weak and lightheaded, when Kayo bustled in. "Jonas, my God, what have you done?"

"I guess you mean the preacher."

"What did you say to him?"

Jonas told him.

"Well, he went straight from here to Fleetwood Satterfield's office. Jonas, that man has a big following, and he thinks he's here to save Copernicus from sinful ruin. Shows up at nearly every Council meeting, worked up about one thing and another." He took a breath. "The mayor was mortified. He's got one pissed-off preacher on his hands. And the preacher's demanding…"

Jonas cut him off. "Chief, I'm gonna save you the trouble. I quit."

Wilma, the home healthcare nurse, was there when he got to the house. Gladys was away at some kind of school function and she had asked him to stay with Rodney.

"He's been awfully agitated," Wilma said. "I tried to get him to write it down on his pad, but he wouldn't. Maybe you can get him calmed down."

Back in the bedroom, Rodney looked more wasted than ever — shriveled and imploding, color all but gone from his face. It wouldn't be long. But Rodney's eyes were wide and intense and his mouth twisted into what might have been an attempt to speak.

"Wilma says you're upset," Jonas said.

Rodney nodded. Then he made a motion with his head toward the notepad and pencil on the bedside table. Jonas handed them to him and he hunched over the pad, hand gripping the pencil so hard Jonas thought it might break. He scratched at the pad, sweat popping out on his forehead, grunting with the effort. Jonas waited. And then he was done. He looked up at Jonas, eyes fierce and burning. Jonas picked up the pad and looked.

DOC U FTR

It took Jonas a moment to decipher, and then he felt a thunderous blow to the pit of his stomach and all the air rushed out of him and the notepad fell from his hands. He stumbled backward into a chair, brain on fire — noise, flame, explosions. He stared at Rodney, saw tears streaming down his face. And that was the last thing he knew for a long time.

* * * * *

He didn't know where he was. Or how he got there. Or when. He was all inside his mind, and everything else was somewhere else, if it existed at all. He was, he realized, searching for himself. Maybe had been forever. He thought that the inside of his mind was a great contradiction — a space small enough that only a mind could fit, but large enough that he could wander about, follow unmarked paths, look for clues. There didn't seem to be any, not yet. But he thought if he was patient...

But at long last patience ran out and he opened his mind's window and saw, when the film over his eyes faded a bit, that he was in his back yard, sprawled in one of the Adirondacks. He looked down. At his bare feet, a jumble of empty beer bottles, another half-empty in his hand. He looked around, tried to focus. He was wearing nothing but boxers and sweat. Nearly dark, the faintest of light fading beyond the trees. Light on in the kitchen. He couldn't remember being there.

He lifted the beer bottle to his lips, gagged, tossed it away, tried to rise, toppled into the grass, feeling every blade of it slicing flesh. He lay still, eyes squeezed shut but with every nerve in his body zinging. Tried to make some sense of it. Then he thought, *What if there is no sense to it, any of it? What if it's all just nonsense? If it is, I'm nonsense too.*

After a long time he slowly opened his eyes again and saw someone standing in the shadows at the edge of the yard, looking at him. And then there were others, and he could feel them moving, pressing in around him. The platoon. The warriors. He felt the old, abiding terror of being in their company, not a fear for his own existence, but for theirs. He cried out to them:

People are trying to kill you, and you never know when or how they might succeed — rip the life out of you and blow it clean out your ass. And when they try, and it comes down to me, I might fail you, let you slip through my fingers because I forgot something or did something wrong or just didn't try hard enough. And then I would forever see your accusing faces and forever feel the life slipping from your ravaged bodies and pay and pay and pay.

He sobbed with rage and desperation and they just kept standing there, so close he might, if he dared, reach and touch them. He could see them all plainly, every single one of them — the ones who lived and the ones who died. He waited for their bitter words, but none came. They all seemed resigned to whatever had happened.

He looked into their haunted eyes and then it all — every horrible detail — came back.

* * * * *

It was a stretch to call it a street — so narrow that it was not much more than an alley between crumpled walls of what had once been dwellings before artillery and mortars had wrecked it. They were two abreast, staying close to the shattered edges of the street, everybody jacked-up and bug-eyed, eyes darting and sweeping, trying to spot what might kill you and the others before it had a chance to. The whole area had been blasted by the horrific sounds of battle the day before, but now it was so quiet the pounding of your heart was like a bass drum in your ears, thu-thump, thu-thump, thu-thump, so loud you couldn't even hear the crunch your boots made on the dirt when you took a step.

Lashley, who they called Pap because he was twenty-eight and had a wife and two kids off-base at LeJeune, was at point with a metal detector, keeping an eye out for disturbed earth that might conceal an IED. Sergeant Willis was maybe twenty yards behind. They came to a place where the street took a right angle, and you couldn't see past it because of a big pile of rubble where a dwelling had once been. Pap eased up to the edge of the pile and peeked around and then looked back at Willis and motioned him forward. Willis threw up a hand and everybody went into a crouch while Willis went to see. Jonas was at the middle of the platoon, just ahead of Lieutenant Hammer, who almost knocked him over as he scurried past, staying low, headed for Willis and Pap. By the time he got to the corner, Willis had taken a look, and then Hammer did too. Willis had a map and he and Hammer knelt over it. The rest of them were watching, eyes darting back and forth from Hammer and Willis to the blasted buildings around them, and then they realized that Hammer and Willis were having an argument, keeping their voices low, Hammer pointing at the corner and Willis shaking his head. It went on for maybe thirty seconds, and then Hammer raised up and went into what they had come to recognize as his linebacker stance. Willis looked up at him for a moment, then folded the map, taking a lot of time at it. He stood, squared his shoulders, stuck the map in a pocket, took a long look at Hammer, then raised his arm and motioned the rest of them forward.

It was after they got around the corner that they saw the car, a burned-out wreck, blackened and twisted by whatever had killed it, skewed sideways so that they had to go single file to pass on one side. Hammer stayed up front with Willis and Pap, and they and maybe six or seven others had passed the car by the time Jonas rounded the corner and saw that the street lay long and ruined in front of them, with a mostly-intact building down at the end, a shred of what must have once been a curtain fluttering from one of the blown-out windows. And then somebody appeared in the window with a grenade launcher, and before anybody could react, the street blew up.

The car was booby-trapped, but that wasn't what set things off. It was the RPG that came screaming up the street, missing Hammer and the other guys up front, but smacking into the car and adding its own explosive to whatever was hidden in the car. The car disintegrated into flying chunks of metal. Lieutenant Hammer turned to look back at his platoon, just in time for one of the chunks to turn his head into a visceral mist. The street erupted in chaos. A lot of people got hit by pieces of the car. There was the ear-shattering sound of the grenade hitting metal, and right with it the walloping concussion, and everybody had his brain rattled around in his skull, leaving a profound absence of anything resembling existence for an instant until it all came back, a thundering wall of sound and blood and pieces of bodies flying apart

Jonas felt himself picked up and then smashed to earth and he lay there in the midst of the chaos, paralyzed by the force of it and then feeling his lungs fighting for air, and after that, bit by agonizing bit, realizing he wasn't hit. He began to strain against himself, willing some kind of movement, anything, failing but then finally rolling over to all fours. He forced himself to look around, but with the smoke and dust and blood in his eyes, he couldn't see much. One hand went instinctively to his back and that was when he realized his assault pack with all of his medical stuff was missing. The next thing was the nasty snapping sound, small arms fire, coming from everywhere. Behind him, he heard somebody cry out as he got hit.

He stumbled to his feet, tottering, trying to get enough balance to move, beginning to see enough now to know how bad it was. He heard screams out there in front where Willis and the head of the platoon were. He took a step, toppled, got up, took another and another. The small arms fire was intense, ripping the air and smacking into things around him. Behind, he heard Dunhill scream, "Return fire!" and after a moment there was the sound of one weapon, then another, firing on automatic, the platoon coming to life, instinct and training taking over. Ahead, the screams, and Jonas kept moving toward them, past where the car had been. He saw what was left of Lieutenant Hammer and what was left of Pap, and beyond them, Marines sprawled in the dirt, maybe some of them still alive. He was seized by terror, of what was out there and what was needed. "I can't do this!" something screeched inside his head, but then there was another voice that said, "I can do this if I lose myself." And he did. Even when they shot him — twice — he did.

* * * * *

And then it was over. It took a long time, well into darkness, before he became aware of anything. Smell of earth and grass and beer. He retched, coming apart inside and spilling what had to be his last piece of humanity into the grass. When it finally passed he pulled himself to his knees, tried to focus. And then he saw that they were all still there, but they were moving away from him, back toward the darkness.

He remembered again the moment there in the street in the village when he faced the certainty of his own death, but was driven by a desperate need to act, to *not fail*. And now that he had finally remembered all of it, he knew that he had not.

FIFTEEN

When he finally woke, it seemed he had lived — and died — through several lifetimes. He felt ancient and used-up and devoid of feeling. He thought that was okay, because he had had quite enough of feeling.

He was in a room in a bed. Okinawa Motel in Jacksonville, blasted back through days and weeks and years to that wretched time when he had cowered from the world, drenched in Ray Willis's blood and brains. And there was Doc, just as before. But no, this wasn't the Okinawa Motel. It was his old room upstairs at Doc's house. He blinked, but Doc was still there in a chair next to the bed, watching him.

"How long…"

"Two days," Doc said.

And then he remembered the street and the chaos and the bodies and his own flesh being torn. And he began to cry.

Doc put a cool hand on his forehead.

"I…" but nothing else would come out. Either it was all still there inside him, feverish and festering or…

"You told me," Doc said. "You told me the whole story. You got it out, and now I have it and you don't have to go back there any more."

He lay there quiet and empty for a time and then he felt Doc's hand on his forehead and remembered what had lit the match and blasted him into the hell of that village.

"You're my father," he said.

"Yes."

And then it swept over him, the memory of all that had gone before that street in the village. The days and years of Rodney, of feeling small and helpless and afraid. "Why? Why didn't you save me?"

"Rest awhile longer," Doc said. "Then we'll talk."

Faint light at the window, end of day. He pulled back the sheet, managed to get his legs swung over the side of the bed, sat there for a long moment feeling faint and drained. It took awhile before he could stand, wobbly, holding onto the bedpost while he got some semblance of balance. He found shorts and tee shirt — washed and folded neatly — on the desk. Pulled them on. His head swam from the effort, but he took his time, gathered himself as best he could, before he started for the door.

Doc was feeding the koi. They rose toward his outstretched hand, roiling the water. The movement made Jonas nauseous and he looked away, sat gingerly in one of the Adirondacks. Doc finished, took the other chair, took a short pull on the Scotch sitting on the armrest. Neither said a word for a minute or two.

Finally. "Your mother told me. She found the notepad, the last thing Rodney ever did.'

"Tell me," Jonas said.

Doc looked him in the eye. "A thousand times I wanted to, and then hoped I never would have to. But now I will."

It began in the days after Gordon Laycock's fraud had been exposed, when Gladys was bereft and ashamed and in desperate need of someone who didn't judge, simply comforted. They had been friends for a long time, but then it became much more, and it remained so even for a short time after Rodney Boulware. Evelyn Ainsley was in the throes of her long, terrible battle with cancer, and Doc wouldn't leave her. So she married Rodney, and they tried to keep each other at arm's length, but they couldn't — that is, until Jonas.

"You said you couldn't have children," Jonas said.

"I said *we* couldn't. But I could."

After Jonas's birth, they broke it off, and that might have been the end of it. But Rodney wanted another child, and when that didn't happen, he finally went to a doctor in another town and got tested. He was sterile. And somehow, he figured it out.

Jonas felt the nausea rising again, despair at the thought of those years of Rodney — the disdain, the belittling, the anger, the disgust. That made sense, coming from a cuckolded man, except for the cruelty of it.

"How could you, the two of you, let me go through that?"

"He threatened to humiliate her," Doc said. "She believed him. I begged her to tell you. After Evelyn died, I begged her to leave him and marry me. But she couldn't."

"I should hate you both," Jonas whispered.

Doc nodded. "You should. You have every right."

"And then what?"

"That's something you'll have to figure out for yourself." He paused, and even in the fading twilight, Jonas could see the glistening of his eyes. "You asked me one time if I ever failed, and I told you about the kid down the street I couldn't save. That was a one-time thing. But for the twenty-one years of your life, I've faced that failure every day. I have failed you miserably for every one of those days, and all I can say now is that I'm profoundly sorry I failed you. I don't know if you can ever forgive that, or if I can ever forgive myself." He paused, running his hand over his thinning scalp. "But this is not about me, it's about you. And the hope I have for you is that you won't let any of this," his hand swept the air between them, marking the time and space of Jonas's life, and his, "keep you from rescuing your life. Don't let other people's mistakes, other people's sins, drag you down."

* * * * *

Doc was wrong, he thought. I do have to go back there again — back to the village and all that came before it and after, back into dark passages that reeked with foul air and wasting flesh.

Carl agreed. "You've reached a point that some never do," he said. "Some only get the bad shit in bits and pieces, striking whenever they let their guard down. So they make a superhuman effort to never let their guard down. And finally it's just too much. And we lose them."

"You've lost some."

"Yes."

"So now what?"

"It depends on how you look at things. Head on, at an angle, but looking nevertheless."

"Will it ever be over?"

"I wish I could say yes, but the great odds are it won't be, not completely. It's part of who you are. You're an intelligent and empathetic young man. You've learned throughout your life that when you care, you make yourself vulnerable. The goal is to keep your caring and compassion, because that's the essence of who you are, not all the other. Dig down and find those best parts of yourself, Jonas. When you do, you can put all the rest in its place."

* * * * *

He didn't see Gladys until the funeral.

Rodney's casket had been open at the altar rail, but when one of the undertaker's people asked him if he wanted a last look, he stared at the man as if he had lost his mind. Doc was at his elbow. He gripped Jonas's arm and gave a firm shake of his head to the undertaker's guy who left them alone and went to close the casket.

Then Gladys was there, standing just beyond his reach with a look that was both quizzical and — he thought — terrified. He looked into her eyes for a long moment, thinking again what he had thought so often in the past few days: *I thought I knew her. My mother, for God's sake. Toting the great weight of family shame on her shoulders, doing abject penance over and over until it seemed that it made her bleed. But family shame was only part of it, maybe not even the most of it. She has known great passion and great risk and, hopefully, even some joy peeking out from behind her wall of secrets. She may be the bravest person I know.*

He hugged her, held onto her for awhile, and then they — Jonas, Gladys and Doc — walked to the front of the church and sat together while the minister said the words.

* * * * *

At the house, after, he endured the smothering feeling of the crowd, the hands, the hugs, the quiet voices, for as long as he could stand it, and then he escaped through the kitchen to the back patio. When the last of them had gone, that's where Doc and Gladys found him, Gladys with a tray of iced tea glasses, Doc carrying the dog, which he handed to Gladys after she had served the tea. They said nothing for a long time.

And then Gladys said, "The District Attorney was here."

Jonas waited, puzzled.

"He's not going to bring charges against Ben."

She looked to Doc, who said, "Clear case of self defense. Ben has been through too much in his young life to put him through anything more."

Jonas felt a rush of relief and hope. *Maybe...* "So could he...?

"Come here?" Gladys said, "Yes."

He stared open-mouthed. "What are you talking about?"

She looked at Doc again. "We've been talking to Social Services," he said. "Ben has two close relatives here — his grandmother and his uncle. If they work together, they can give Ben a safe, stable, loving home. So it depends on whether this grandmother and this uncle think they can pull it off."

"My God," Jonas said softly.

"My money," Doc said with a hint of a smile, "is on the grandmother and the uncle."

Jonas sat there stunned for a long time while Doc sipped on his iced tea and Gladys ruffled the dog's hair. And then Jonas stood up, setting his glass back on the tray. "Then let's go get Ben out of that goddamned jail."

He called Lieutenant the next morning. "I need a job."

"How soon can you be here?"

"Give me a couple of days. Some stuff I need to work on."

"Whenever you're ready," Lieutenant said. Then, "I talked to Doc."

"You know."

"All of it." A long silence and then Lieutenant said, "Doc is as good a man as I've ever known. You're a lot like him. Let him be there for you. Make up for lost time."

"You're right about Doc," Jonas said. "I will."

Doc said, "There's money if you want to go to school."

"I haven't thought about it. A lot of other things on my mind."

"Of course. But think about it. Start with community college, then something in medicine. Physician Assistant, maybe."

"I don't know if I could do that, Doc."

"A lot of choices, different kinds of choices, ahead of you," Doc said. "But I know this: you are meant to pass through this world caring for people. God help you."

* * * * *

He was halfway home when Fred Wesley's truck pulled up to the curb and Fred Wesley leaned out the window. "Christy Jo and I want you to come to supper."

"Supper, huh?"

"Christy Jo's stir-fry has got a lot better. We have spaghetti one night, stir-fry the next. Tonight's stir-fry."

"I'd be honored, Fred Wesley. What can I bring?"

"Yourself. That'll be plenty enough."

When he got home from Fred Wesley's he sat down at the kitchen table and opened the notebook he had bought at the convenience store and took ballpoint pen in hand. He had thought about using a pencil, but he didn't want to erase anything, and he wanted it all down where he could see it plainly. He took a deep breath and then wrote,

Once upon a time there was a street in a village.

THE END

Robert Inman is a native of Elba, Alabama and a graduate of The University of Alabama with a Master of Fine Arts degree in Creative Writing. He left a 30-year career in television news in 1996 to devote full time to his writing career.

In addition to his work as a novelist, he is the author of six motion pictures for television and eight published stage plays, including two musicals. Two of his motion pictures have been "Hallmark Hall of Fame" presentations.

Inman and his wife Paulette live in Franklin, TN. They have two daughters, Larkin Ferris of Wilmington, NC and Lee Farabaugh of Franklin.

Author's website: www.robert-inman.com.

www.ingramcontent.com/pod-product-compliance
Lightning Source LLC
Chambersburg PA
CBHW030525020726
47494CB00004B/1241